"They look a little like me," said R'ya critically. "I suppose they will have to do. I don't like the way they are dividing up the kill with their fore-limbs. We'll have to teach them how to use the food synthesizer immediately."

One complete, live specimen, rather young and a little smaller than R'ya, snarled at them from a corner of the control room, locked in a light stasis cage.

"His personality . . . ," began her robot Tec.

"I'm going to call him Uru, and he's all mine. You'll see, Tec. Uru will be my mate and my weapon against the Roiiss. A living weapon."

The fifty-foot Tyrannosaurus rex stared back at them with malevolence in his reptilian eyes.

The
SECOND
EXPERIMENT

J. O. Jeppson

A FAWCETT CREST BOOK

Fawcett Publications, Inc., Greenwich, Connecticut

THE SECOND EXPERIMENT

THIS BOOK CONTAINS THE COMPLETE TEXT OF THE
ORIGINAL HARDCOVER EDITION.

A Fawcett Crest Book reprinted by arrangement with
Houghton Mifflin Company

ISBN 0-449-23005-8

Printed in the United States of America

10 9 8 7 6 5 4 3 2 1

CONTENTS

To Isaac with love

SOURCE

OF ERROR

1

Tec stood alone in deep shadow at the garden's edge, while before him rose the great golden helix of the Tower of History, its top glowing with light as dawn came to Roiissa.

Curiosity marks the sentient being, and mystery arouses desire for knowledge, even forbidden knowledge. Tec made his decision.

I want to go inside, he thought, looking up at the Tower. Behind him, the sea of blooms he tended so carefully was opening for pollination by the morning air currents.

The curiosity of even a small sentient being can put in motion events which may reach cosmic dimensions, but there was no one to tell Tec that. The only other intelligent life forms on the planet were the Roiiss, who were absorbed in that unending problem they called the Second Experiment. They had not bothered to speak to Tec for years, possibly because they did not consider him to be intelligent or alive. It was true that he was not composed of molecules capable of reproduction.

"But living things have other properties," muttered Tec stubbornly. "I am responsive and aware." He was not fully aware of just how stubborn he was.

He had been gardener for the Roiiss for so long that he automatically looked back, noticing that yet another seedling had managed to implant itself upon the enormous statue of an ancient Roiiss that looked as if it had once fallen, inexplicably and carelessly, yet never been restored.

He was supposed to keep the statue clear, which was difficult when he delighted in the growth of all life, but he was not going to garden today.

Moving silently through the waning shadow while fear surged through his emotive centers, Tec stealthily opened the mammoth door of the adjoining building, the never used Palace of the Roiiss. Inside, the great domed ceiling of the Council Chamber glittered with jewels. The five thrones were also jeweled, and empty. The five stern portraits of the Roiiss Elders looked down at Tec as if they watched his every move. Many times before Tec's curiosity had been inhibited by those portraits, so this time he looked down at the map of the Home solar system shining from delicate mosaics in the Chamber floor.

The only door to the Tower of History was at the far end of the Council Chamber. It was locked. Once Tec had dared to ask if he might be permitted to go in.

"You are permitted no further knowledge" had been the thundered reply.

It held him up for a few years, but it also taught him that the Tower must contain much information, a supposition which worked its way deep into the curiosity part of his emotive centers. Knowledge—was it the key to pleasure, power, defeat of boredom?

And I want to know what I am, thought Tec as he hovered before the Tower door. He was not equipped with built-in offensive weapons, but he had delicate mechanisms for operating his hands and a mind that could tune in to the distress of a flower. The lock's mechanism could not remain a mystery forever, although Tec was quite prepared to take that long. He concentrated.

Four hours later the door opened and the Elders caught him.

"Remain where you are, robot."

They were terrifying. They always had been, and were getting more so.

"In case you've forgotten," he said, "my name is Tec, and I haven't much to do so I thought . . ."

"You are not supposed to think."

"But I can't help it!"

"Silence!"

Tec knew they were powerful. He hovered in the open doorway with his built-in antigravity mechanism, swiveling his head so he could watch all five of them with his wide golden eyes. They would undoubtedly talk about him, telepathically. Now that the Roiiss were immortal, they seldom bothered to use ordinary speech, except to give orders to his lesser mind, just as they hardly ever took the old protoplasmic shape. They drifted through the Council Chamber like five portions of multicolored smoke, beautiful and dangerous.

"What shall we do with him?"

Tec's impassive, metallic face registered no emotion, but his emotive centers gyrated. He could hear them! Not hear through auditory devices, but in his mind. The intense concentration induced by the problem of the lock and the fear of the Roiiss had awakened telepathic powers. He would certainly not inform the Roiiss. Instead, he listened:

"He must not be allowed to enter the Tower."

"What difference can it make?"

"Why does he want to acquire knowledge?"

"Apparently he wants something to do besides gardening."

"Perhaps he is insane."

"Don't you remember how he was originally programmed? He was the only one given emotive centers and curiosity. Intelligence alone might give a need for power, but he has other needs."

There was a pause. Tec wondered if the Roiiss were remembering some distant past when they, too, were intensely curious, given to boredom with easy work that did not use their mental capacities.

"We planned to activate him immediately after the successful conclusion of the First Experiment, upon our arrival in this solar system . . ."

"But we were so busy thinking about the Second Experiment . . ."

"Then we wanted the garden, and later he was the only one . . ."

"And after a while we didn't want to be distracted. His original programming cannot be carried out now."

"Yet we had promised those we left behind on the Home planet . . ."

"Yes, we promised."

Tec sensed their sudden grief in remembering the loss of the Home planet, but their minds turned quickly back to logical problems. In a dangerous universe the Roiiss had tried to give up any passion, except that for survival.

"Whatever he does will not really interfere with our work."

"He will not take part in the Second Experiment."

"He will not survive. We will."

"And we can always destroy him."

They were silent, as if each one contemplated the best way of killing him. In spite of mounting horror, Tec could not stop his own thoughts from turning to a foolproof way. He knew he was virtually indestructible, but he was certain that if ordered to plunge himself into Roiissa's sun, he would become most effectively deactivated.

Tec had never met another robot. No one had told him that an ordinary robot's primary function is to obey the orders of his masters, not to question them.

"I won't destroy myself," he said inside his head. "And maybe I'll try to stop them from killing me." He looked steadily at the swirling patterns, now coalescing into one shape vaguely reminiscent of the protoplasmic Roiiss.

He began to feel pressure in his head. No! He would

rather plunge into the sun than have his mind turned off!

"Elders! Whatever you decide to do to punish my arrogance in trying to enter the Tower, please remember that I may become necessary to you someday. Are you capable of manipulating mechanical devices now? Are you even able to handle ordinary matter with ease? Surely you might need your only robot in the future."

He sensed their consternation. However intelligent the Roiiss indubitably were, they didn't think of everything. It was a delightful discovery. Yet threatening, because they were angry at the merest hint that they were not all-powerful.

The pressure on his mind increased. They were trying to probe him, and instantly his mindshield went up. He had not known that he possessed one.

"I am an individual," he said to himself grimly. "I have a right to the privacy of my own mind."

"His mind is too thick to probe."

"Probably too unintelligent, in spite of what he just said."

Tec waved one arm in a deprecating manner. "Oh magnificent ones, please allow me to serve your great power. My function is to serve. My emotive centers bind me to the welfare of the mighty Roiiss."

"It's true that a robot might continue to be useful."

"We might need him for phases of the Second Experiment."

"He might as well start educating himself in basic technology, since it is unfortunately true that we are losing our ability to manipulate ordinary matter. Let him enter the Tower."

"Yes, let him. After all, we agree that we can always kill him."

The phantom Roiiss shape dissolved into five. They stared at Tec balefully.

"You have our permission to study in the Tower. The

underground library contains information on basic science and technology. The laboratory is self-explanatory. The Tower of History shows you a record of past events, which need no verbal explanation if you are intelligent enough, and which cannot be explained if you are not. When puzzled by anything in the Tower, do not ask questions. There will be no one here to answer, and we do not wish to be bothered again."

"But I . . ."

"If you should perchance acquire knowledge that makes you afraid, that is your problem. The Roiiss search for their own solutions. You must do the same."

As they drifted out of the Council Chamber, Tec caught one last telepathic remark.

"He will never grasp the meaning of section two."

In the entrance hall of the Tower of History, hidden lamps turned on as soon as he entered, lighting the ramp of the helix as it curved gently upward. Once the Roiiss had intended to walk up that ramp to gaze upon their own history, or had it been meant for someone else? Tec turned off his antigrav. He would walk, too.

The walls became alive with pictures as soon as he started up the ramp. The images were identical on each side, changing as he went forward. At first he was mystified at the seething chaos he saw, wondering what it symbolized, when he began to recognize some of the forming shapes as collections of stars called galaxies. The pictures became more detailed, showing one particular galaxy, and focused on a solar system identical to that on the Council Chamber floor.

He had never thought about it before, but he realized that his mind had once been programmed with all sorts of information, or he wouldn't have been able to recognize a galaxy. They were islands of billions of stars, and there were billions of galaxies scattered throughout the universe. Stars in the galaxies often had planets forming solar systems.

The pictures focused on one planet of the Home solar system, and Tec saw that its seas were much larger than those of Roiissa. In those seas, life was beginning. Weird, primitive life that ate and was eaten, died and became part of new life evolving gradually with growing complexity, diversity, and a ferocious determination for survival. The pictures were marvelous, almost breathing on the wall. They frightened Tec a little, but he was certainly not bored; then he thought he must have been bored for years, perhaps because so little ever happened. The Roiiss drifted, planning their Second Experiment; the garden grew and the statue had to be cleaned, but life had been dully the same for as long as Tec could remember. Now he was going to learn. Awareness without knowledge, without increasing use of itself, is frustrating.

In the pictures, some life moved out of the seas of the Home planet onto dry land, into every possible niche for existence. The multitude of forms bewildered Tec, for on Roiissa there were only the Roiiss and the wind-pollinated vegetation, but he liked the diversity because it offered so many interesting, aesthetically satisfying possibilities for life to explore. Then he saw a shape vaguely familiar. Not quite a Roiiss, but almost.

There! The first Roiiss, walking erect, in a world still primitive beyond Tec's comprehension. The gradual curve of the great Tower drew him on, walking past the early development of the creatures now called Roiiss, into his own destiny.

"Survival," muttered Tec as he stared at the walls. "How they fought for it." The Roiiss had once been unimaginably fierce. How much of that was left in them now? He thought that perhaps he'd better not find out.

Gradually the Roiiss changed, not in form but in behavior. They experimented, learned, developed civilizations of many kinds. They fought each other until it seemed as if there would be no Roiiss, possibly no planet left. Yet the instinct for survival remained paramount, saving them from self-destruction. So many other creatures did not survive as the Roiiss dominated the Home planet. Tec, a nurturer of life, grieved for those creatures. He knew only too well how the Roiiss held beings other than themselves in contempt. The ecology of the Home planet was thrown out of balance, and yet the Roiiss continued to pollute and overpopulate.

Then, with a last heroic effort, the Roiiss united, ventured into space and built a galactic empire with the help of—

"Like me! Others like me!"

Shining, cylindrical creatures working for the Roiiss— duplicates of Tec. "Why wasn't I told? I've always thought I was the only one. I've never had someone like myself to talk to."

In the pictures robots accompanied the Roiiss in all the later stages of their technological development reaching across their galaxy. The robots looked indispensible. What had happened to them? Was he the only one left?

Something was going wrong in the pictures. The Roiiss were afraid, desperately afraid. He had no way of judging what had caused it, or how long it took for the fear to grow.

Roiiss and their robots gathered in huge meetings and, under pressure, they seemed to be developing telepathy, with billions of minds working together to combat some terrible danger. The best of the Roiiss minds went back to the Home planet, turned into a giant laboratory for experimentation—on what?

"Why?" asked Tec to the silence. "What was wrong? Why are the pictures not more explicit?" But he thought he knew the answer to the last question. The Roiiss were afraid of everything not like themselves. Had they not chosen to come to Roiissa, a planet devoid of other animal life, to start the Second Experiment? They believed they had no hope of help from anyone but themselves, perhaps because they alone had had to escape whatever danger led to the First Experiment. They isolated themselves in their grim need to wrest certainty out of uncertainty.

Illumination in the curving corridor was increasing, an intense glow radiating from the walls. Tec had to lower his secondary eyelids for protection of his visual apparatus. He peered at the pictures, trying to understand. It looked as if the Roiiss had learned how to control and transmute matter and energy. They even increased their psi powers to be able to alter physical structure, curing disease and deformity. Perhaps the present Roiiss ability to dissolve their shapes completely came from that.

They had invented longevity medicine, antigravity, and hyperspace drive long before. Now they were building the final starship, part of the First Experiment. Pictures showed the interior of a magnificently engineered ship.

Most of the Roiiss started to die from radiation that seemed to be increasing throughout their galaxy. Most of the robots turned themselves off rather than suffer aberrations of their minds from brain damage. Roiiss embryos with the best genetic equipment were placed in a stasis container with a silver pentagram on it and Tec wondered if this represented the five Elders, perhaps carried as embryos on whatever journey the spaceship made. Certainly the Elders were the epitome of Roiiss superiority, with unimaginable power.

Yet Tec was quite sure that there were more than five Roiiss on the planet Roiissa. Were the others those who had brought the embryos, or were they the children of the Roiiss? Perhaps the Tower of History had been built for the instruction of the children. Then why were there no more young Roiiss?

The light was blinding. Tec bumped into the end of

the corridor before he realized that it was closed off. Hastily, eager to get out of section one, he opened the door in the obstructive wall.

It was so dark inside that Tec turned on his infrared vision, but he saw nothing on the walls. As he moved slowly, carefully through section two, he began to experience an eerie tingling, a feeling of immense pressure, a sensation of imminent catastrophe.

Suddenly he was terrified. He had always been more or less alone, but the conviction of utter, absolute aloneness had never before entered his consciousness. His mind shuddered with fear; he knew now with complete certainty that each individual mind in the universe is fundamentally alone, facing its own destiny no matter who or what tries to share the journey, each bearing total responsibility for its own awareness and its own life.

The ancient Roiiss had been able to weep. Tec longed for the release of tears.

He fled to the next door, into section three. It was conventionally lighted, a simple, short part of the Tower containing an open, six-foot high glass container and a model of the planet Roiissa. This was the end of the First Experiment—the successful journey to Roiissa, far from the dangers attacking the Home planet and its colonies. Or was it far enough? Was that the dilemma leading to the Second Experiment? Was that why the Roiiss did not enjoy life, but worked only toward future survival?

He went over to the glass case. A small label at the base read TEC.

They had brought him to Roiissa in this case, unactivated. Why? Was he only a gardener?

This seemed to be the end of the Tower. Was he to go back down the same way? He didn't want to go into section two again. He moved close to the walls, looking for a way out, and saw a well-hidden door, the seams almost invisible in the slight undulations of the walls. He pressed against it, and it creaked open reluctantly.

Now he was at the top of the Tower, a huge room with walls stretching up to a high vaulted ceiling. He was about to turn on his infrared again, for it was dark, when a circle of light began to widen at the top. The Tower was opening to daylight like a flower.

Then he saw the bodies. Thousands of them—distorted, dismembered, decapitated, heads smashed beyond recognition. These were his fellow robots, those who had been activated before the journey to Roiissa, who had built the Palace and laid out the garden that Tec tended. Not one was repairable.

In the center of the room on a low table was a stasis box marked by a silver pentagram. Had the robots been punished for not giving the embryo Roiiss proper care? The Roiiss living on the planet Roiissa were enormously different from those who prepared the First Experiment on the Home planet.

Tec opened the box. The embryo tubes were still inside, full—

At that moment the noonday sun burst into the open top of the Tower, rays ricocheting from the multifaceted sloping walls covered with polished metal which shone like a mirror.

Tec looked up at dazzling reflections of himself, hundreds of Tec from all angles.

He accepted without surprise the fact that there was a silver pentagram on the top of his own head.

He picked up the embryo container and rose on antigrav to the opening of the Tower.

2

The Empire is dead.
The Roiiss continue.
Tribe of Tribes, First of the First.
Survival beyond survival.
The Roiiss continue.

R'ya chanted the ancient litany with obvious displeasure, which Tec pretended not to notice. His job, he kept telling himself, was to educate the only child of the ancient Roiiss. It was a pity she had to learn the old chants. They only made her more aware of the fact that none of the other embryos had lived to be her mate, and that the Elders were interested only in their own survival, not hers. At least the Elders had not stopped Tec from growing the one healthy embryo.

"I hate the elders," said R'ya, stamping her foot. "None of them even look at me. And I'm beautiful, the most beautiful of all the Roiiss. Isn't that so, Tec?"

"Beauty is not an absolute," said Tec, looking away from her and wishing he were a Roiiss instead of a robot. "Beauty is a concept which depends on who defines it."

"Then I have to find someone who thinks I'm beautiful, is that it?"

"Yes, R'ya."

It was a fatal reply.

R'ya was in late adolescence. Up to now, Tec had enjoyed almost every minute of his surrogate parenthood. The "almost" was the time he spent worrying about whether or not the Roiiss would take R'ya with them when they left to complete their Second Experiment. He still had not found out what the Second Experiment was, but the Roiiss had said that eventually they would leave. He wanted them to accept R'ya as their child, for her sake, yet the hope that she would stay with him hovered near the surface of his mind all the time, in spite of his constant attempts to push it under.

He had taught himself and R'ya everything in the Roiissan library, but he had not told her that it was obvious many bits of information had been removed. There was nothing about the First Experiment, or about the journey to Roiissa, or even about what happened to the ship that landed there. Now and then he tried to talk to the Elders.

"Bah, we should not have given you the emotive centers necessary to your original programming."

"I wish you would take them away," said Tec in his more suffering moments.

"That is impossible."

"Please take R'ya—and me—with you when you go."

"We can survive. You and the child will be a hindrance."

"Take her in stasis. She is the last of the old Roiiss."

"A throwback who clutters our thinking with useless questions and pleas for attention. She is vain about the beauty of her shape, refusing to learn matter control. She is poor at telepathy. We find her to be an irritant, unsuited for our life now."

"But she will change," said Tec. "She is young, capable of maturing."

"The First Experiment changed us beyond recall, and we go on changing ourselves to prepare for the Second. R'ya is more like you than like us as we are now. We are sorry."

Tec thought that perhaps there was a vestige of pity left in the Roiiss, enough to keep them from killing R'ya and himself, but he was not sure. The differences between

R'ya and the Elders grew constantly, and the Elders despised anything different.

One day R'ya burst into the laboratory where Tec was studying antigravity.

"You must build a ship, Tec. You must take me to another planet where I can find a mate."

"I'll try," said Tec, knowing that the hyperspace formulas for faster-than-light drive had been deleted from the library, and that he had not yet figured them out, much less built a ship. He returned to the first section of the Tower, hoping to get some clue from the murals. Surely the Roiiss wouldn't want to forget the formulas. Perhaps the mathematics was hidden in the design somewhere. As he studied the pictures, finding no hint, R'ya joined him, impatient.

"Silly pictures," she said. "The Home planet probably wasn't nearly as nice as Roiissa. Why do the Elders want to leave? And look at the way they used to be—just like me, only not as perfect. Why can't they appreciate me? I went out to dance for them, and they just disappeared. I know I'm graceful. Look how stiff the pictures are— especially that one," she said, pointing to a stylized design of a Roiiss about to leap up into the unknown.

"It looks like the statue in the garden," mused Tec.

"That moldy old thing?"

"Yes, but here it's standing on end—R'ya! That's the ship, the one they came in! They made their last spaceship look like themselves!"

Late that night, while R'ya insured the absence of the Elders by singing and dancing upon the giant prone statue in the garden, Tec dug his way to the airlock. His mind reached out to the mechanism, understood it, and he opened the door.

"It's really a ship!" said R'ya.

"A magnificent ship," said Tec, finding that his robot emotive centers were responsive to Roiiss machinery as well as to Roiiss females. "But get in, R'ya. Hurry."

"Can it go?" asked R'ya, jealously. She scrambled inside.

"I think it had better. I sense the presence of the Elders nearby. They are angry."

"Tec! thundered the voice, penetrating the hull of the ship or perhaps only searing their minds. "Leave the ship at once! It is forbidden to you."

"They're going to kill us," wailed R'ya.

"The airlock is closed," said Tec, "and the Roiiss can't manipulate machinery very well."

"But they're hurting my mind!" said R'ya, whimpering in pain. "Do something, Tec."

He pushed his mind into the engines, into the ship's computer, into the navigational system. Shutting out R'ya's pain and the threat of the Roiiss, Tec absorbed the essence of the ship into his being. Then he found his hands on the control board.

"Sit down and strap yourself in, R'ya. We're taking off."

He touched a button and the ship lifted, leaving the garden almost intact. A vast presence promptly filled the viewer—the Roiiss, coalesced into one enormous, boiling mass of anger and mental power. Tec tightened his mind-shield.

"Oh, please, Elders," cried R'ya, "don't be angry. We'll come back as soon as I've found a mate. Don't you want —grandchildren?"

There was silence. Tec realized that the Roiiss were probably talking about it while they followed the ship in orbit around Roiissa. He ventured to probe with his own mind, hoping they wouldn't feel it.

"We must not destroy the ship. We may need it."

"But we can't use it without Tec's help now."

"We must grow past the need for a ship."

"Perhaps we should destroy the ship, for with it they might be able to make their own Experiment."

"And that would destroy our plans for the future."

"We must gather our mental powers to kill them, now."

The pain began to bloom in Tec's mind like an evil flower, blotting out thought. He resisted, throwing it back at them.

"Elders!" he called to them telepathically. "There are weapons on this ship. You are not yet so powerful that you can defend yourselves completely against the energies of a spaceship defended by its own field."

"We will become more powerful than you can imagine!" The seething mass in the viewer elongated, lashing in rage.

The pain in Tec's robot brain increased. Did they remember that his programming might prevent him from harming any Roiiss?

"You are no longer Roiiss," he shouted. "Only R'ya commands my loyalty. I will kill you if I can." He hoped they would believe it.

He adjusted the controls. "Elders, hear me well. I am taking R'ya to find an intelligent protoplasmic creature . . ."

"Who will look on me with eyes of love," said R'ya defiantly.

"And when we return," said Tec, "I will destroy you if you threaten R'ya."

As he put the ship into hyperspace, he caught one last thought from the Elders.

"He doesn't know how to use the ship well enough. We may have more time to ourselves than he imagines."

They were lucky, thought Tec as he dipped the ship in and out of hyperspace, jumping across the galaxy in search of intelligent life. He had mastered the normal operation of the ship with ease.

"But why don't you find anyone like me?" said R'ya after the tenth habitable planet had been disappointing.

"Evolution is seldom convergent," said Tec. "Life evolves in many ways, filling every possible niche on every kind of planet that will support life at all. Only rarely would it be likely that a species evolve to resemble another, except in basic functioning. You need someone intelligent enough to appreciate your intelligence, although they may not look anything like you."

"I want both," said R'ya, who was exceedingly determined as well as beautiful. "Those swimming things on that last water planet were awfully bright, but I can't see having a companion that lives in a tank out in the Palace garden. Oh, Tec, I do so want a proper mate. Maybe we'll find the Home planet and other Roiiss like me."

"No, R'ya. I'm sure the Home planet is dead. I suspect that it was not even in this galaxy."

"Will we search other galaxies for Roiiss refugees?"

"Perhaps," said Tec. Yet he was sure that R'ya was the last, just as he was the last of the Roiissan robots.

It was difficult enough to search one galaxy. Hyperspace itself had to be navigated with care, especially near the core of the galaxy where star explosions seemed to have pinched off parts of hyperspace.

"I don't like faster-than-light travel," said R'ya. "Every time you take the ship into hyperspace so we can pop out at some other place far away, I get queasy and have to adjust."

"But you're getting better at it."

"It's no fun at all."

They were past the core of the galaxy now, exploring the spiral arms at the other side of the elongated disc of stars. After another ten planetary explorations, R'ya was indignant.

"There are so many sniveling, smelly bits of crawling protoplasm over this weird galaxy, most of it only fit to be stepped on. Find something that's at least my size."

"We ourselves may seem repulsive to other forms, R'ya."

"You're so smooth and shiny gold you couldn't be repulsive to anything, Tec, and you've told me I'm beautiful, so why shouldn't we be admired most?"

Tec wondered when she would realize that she had a lot to learn. "Beauty in any form is to be admired, theoretically, but it is not necessarily admirable . . ."

"Don't be nasty and intellectual. Isn't that a planet?"

They had emerged near another G-type sun, the stable kind of second generation star most likely to have planets. It had several, in fact, nine. The third definitely had life, so they went down to look at it.

"Quadrupeds," said R'ya scornfully, "and more crawly things."

"Some of the hunting forms are biped," said Tec. "Not very intelligent—no machines, not even agriculture—but more interesting than the herbivores."

They were distracted for a moment by the sudden appearance of a creature which seemed to sail out of the top of a tree, landing in a bush lower down and farther away. Tec had studied flying creatures of the Home planet—there were none on Roiissa—so he explained aerodynamics to R'ya.

"I want wings!"

"Aerodynamically impossible with your size."

"Silly! I'll use my antigrav belt, but have wings for beauty and fun. You can figure out a way to help me change my shape that much. After all, the Elders can change shape at will all the time."

"I don't know," said Tec, "but that reminds me—it might be possible, if we take enough specimens, to do some genetic engineering on the embryos of these hunting creatures to make them more intelligent."

"They look a little like me," said R'ya critically. "I suppose they will have to do. I don't like the way they are dividing up the kill with their forelimbs. We'll have to teach them how to use the food synthesizer immediately."

After appropriate anesthesia and surgery, embryo specimens from many of the hunting bipeds soon filled bottles in the ship's storeroom, preserved in a stasis field.

One complete, live specimen, rather young and a little smaller than R'ya, snarled at them from a corner of the control room, locked in a light stasis cage.

"Isn't he lovely?" said R'ya. "So strong. I'll give him real wings, too. We'll show the Elders what it's like to be real, to be alive."

"His personality . . ." began Tec.

"I'm going to call him Uru, and he's all mine."

Tec looked at Uru with grave doubts in his mind, and then at R'ya. She had never been so radiant. The tip of her tail twitched in eagerness, the iridescent purple scales glittering. She flicked her forked tongue over her lips, past the three rows of pointed teeth. On the five flexible digits, retractable claws sucked in and out, polished to perfection.

"You'll see, Tec. Uru will be my mate and my weapon against the Roiiss. A living weapon."

The fifty-foot *Tyrannosaurus rex* stared back at them with malevolence in his reptilian eyes.

3

"Odd, said Tec.

"What?" asked R'ya, admiring her dragon reflection in the shiny metal door of the control room.

"The ship's instruments indicate some sort of localized distortion in hyperspace here."

"Like the awful parts near the galactic core?"

"No, quite different. It's very much like the thing I noticed when we left Uru's solar system and went back into hyperspace. R'ya, stop teasing the poor creature. It doesn't like the food from our synthesizer as it is."

R'ya was scandalized. "You mean my precious Uru looks at me as food, not as a potential mate?"

"Indubitably. Now listen, R'ya. This is important. I think we've discovered something. When we left Uru's planet, there was a mark like a scar in hyperspace, showing where we'd gone into normal space and come out again."

"What Uru thinks of me is more important."

"Uru doesn't think. Not yet. His descendants will." Tec studied the instruments again. "This localized distortion is another hyperspace scar, only a few light years from Uru's planet. It could mean that some other species has developed hyperspace travel, if ships coming from normal space made that sort of mark."

"Let's go down and look."

The fifth planet of the solar system nearest the hyperspace scar had civilized life—cities, roads, atmospheric flight.

"I don't see any evidence of spaceships," said Tec.

"Oh, Tec, I don't care. I want to go down and visit. This is the first planet we've seen with real cities on it."

"We ought to be cautious," said Tec, whose emotive centers frequently didn't comply. "We'd better stay in orbit and use the language translator for a while."

"We can do that by tuning into their broadcasts," said R'ya, putting the language master on her head. "Ugh. Horrible language. Are you sure they're civilized?"

"The sensors indicate so."

"And protoplasmic?"

He was a trifle hurt, but he wondered if a civilization could be, eventually, entirely robotic. He wondered also what it would be like to know other robots.

"The life here is protoplasmic and carbon based. Except for a few rudimentary silicon based forms, all life in the universe is probably based on carbon due to the natural proclivity of carbon atoms to form complex molecules with each other and with other elements . . ."

"It's the planet Wose," announced R'ya from under the language master. "The natives are Wosians. I can speak it now. Here, Tec, hurry up and learn it. I want to land at once."

The air was breathable, but unpleasantly full of sulphur dioxide, apparently because not only the industries, but also the animal life itself emitted both carbon and sulphur dioxide, which were absorbed by the vegetation.

"Don't eat anything but your own food," warned Tec as they stepped from the airlock. Tec had already deepened the stasis in Uru's cage to keep him asleep, and now he put the ship in a stasis lock. The Wosian radio broadcasts seemed harmless enough, but he was enough of a Roiiss to distrust strangers.

R'ya sneezed. "The air makes my eyes itch. You're

lucky you're a robot, Tec. What's that!"

A little procession of twelve objects emerged from a squatty building on the right, heading for R'ya and Tec. They were decidedly shaggy objects, with several stumpy orange legs protruding from round cushions festooned with long filaments of differing diameters and dubious functions. They also had body odor.

"I believe the thinking organ is possibly that bulge at the back, assuming that the back is what isn't facing us," said Tec. "I think the eyes are on the end of those top stalks."

"They slither," said R'ya, "and smell. Why don't they say something?"

The Wosians arranged themselves in a silent semicircle before their visitors. When Tec tried to probe their minds, it was like venturing into a sea of mud.

"They're not telepathic. I'll speak to them in Wosian. We greet you, honorable Wosians," he began.

The semicircle shuddered and drew into a twitching clump.

"Why does your servant greet us?" they said in unison to R'ya, their voices issuing thickly from unseen apertures.

"Servant?" said R'ya, struggling with the language.

"That machine. Do you disrespect us so much that you insult us with the speech of machines?"

"But you use machines!" said R'ya.

"Our war with machines was over long ago. They never will rise again. We have only our savior, Wirzan."

"R'ya," called Tec telepathically. She hated speaking mind to mind, but had rudimentary use of it. "Don't argue with them. If they distrust me, I will be silent. You talk to them, politely. Ask to see this Wirzan. Remember that we have brought weapons, and you are much bigger than they are. I suspect that they once had a more complex technological civilization, but they seem reasonably intelligent even now. We must meet their leader."

R'ya smiled sweetly at the assembled eyestalks. "Take us to your leader, Wirzan," she said grandly.

A strangled gurgling seemed to indicate consensus—at least on something—for the dozen Wosians beckoned simultaneously with their longest filaments and scurried around to form another clot in back of Tec.

"Onward to the Civic Center," they said, squushing forward. From recesses in their anatomy they extracted short metal rods, which they waved rhythmically as the procession moved into the largest building, a sandy rectangular shape directly ahead.

"Notice the fine examples of Wosian sculpture," they chanted, waving the rods at the entrance hall walls. Mysterious bulges protruding from the dun-colored surfaces revealed themselves as portraits of Wosians, each indistinguishable from any other.

R'ya bumped her head on the ceiling every time she forgot and stood completely upright and again when they went through another doorway to what was possibly a reception room. It was round, had a high vaulted ceiling, was devoid of furniture, and reeked of Wosians, who filled the floor space, except for a small bare circle in the center. A strange arrangement of stringy vegetable matter decorated the ceiling directly over the center. Hanging near this was a small box on the end of a long wire.

"Please step up to the microphone," said the verbal dozen to R'ya, "so that the rest of our people may hear the voice of a visitor from the stars."

"How lovely," said R'ya, stepping carefully between the ranks—spatially and olfactorily—of Wosians on her way to the center of the room.

Tec called to her telepathically. "Wait, R'ya. I've been trying to study some of the mechanical objects with my scanners, and while that hanging box is indeed a microphone, it is plastic. In fact, the only metal I can scan out is in those rods they carry and in the basement of this building. I think these Wosians are descendants of creatures more highly civilized, who used up the sparse metals on this planet, and had spaceships, but for some unknown reason couldn't travel to other planets to replenish their supplies, so their technology collapsed..."

He saw the flash of light from the little metal rods, but his brain had no time to integrate the data before his activity centers were paralyzed. He could see, hear, and think, but he could do nothing, not even elevate on antigrav. As his cylindrical body fell over, he realized with horror that unless R'ya contacted him telepathically, he probably would not be able to communicate with her.

"Tec!" screamed R'ya, turning at the sound of his fall.

The tough fiber netting draped above her head hurtled down to imprison her, the coils tightening as she thrashed.

"Alien," said the Wosians, "you are our prisoner. The Great Wirzan wishes to keep you for inspection and amusement. According to Wirzan's instructions, we have deactivated your robot. His metal will be used for scrap." Tentacles snaked through the netting to remove R'ya's antigrav belt and stun gun, which she was frantically trying to reach.

The original party of twelve Wosians, distinguishable by their metal rods, slithered out of the room. The rest spread out into a large circle hugging the walls, all eye filaments turned toward R'ya. Tec could see her, too, as well as one of the narrow windows through which daylight was obviously waning. No electric lights turned on.

"How can you be so cruel?" gasped R'ya under the constricting web. "How could you have killed my Tec, my friend, my..." she began to sob.

Tec could find no way of getting past the mind block to tell her he was only paralyzed. He felt utterly humiliated.

"We didn't do anything to you," she wailed. "We were only trying to be friendly."

There was no answer. The Wosians went on breathing

out their sulphur and carbon dioxides with sibilant regularity.

"My people will avenge my death! I am R'ya of Roiissa!"

A metallic scraping noise, like a sliding door imperfectly oiled, came from above. The microphone withdrew into the ceiling and emerged again accompanied by a large round ball studded with what Tec knew immediately were sensor organs. The ball was not protoplasmic.

"You will not die, R'ya of Roiissa," said the ball. "I am Wirzan of Wose. I will get information from you."

"The Great Wirzan?" said R'ya, scornfully, squirming under the net to get a good look at the ball.

"I am this entire building," said Wirzan. "I am infinitely more powerful than you and your puny robot. But you have a ship in stasis lock. I want it. Give it to me."

"Only Tec can do that, and you've killed him."

Oh, R'ya, thought Tec, you've signed your death warrant. Wirzen knows I'm alive—he has powerful telepathic powers—but he can't probe your mind very well. He knows how to deal with robots, but not with Roiiss.

"Yes," said Wirzan, his telepathic voice squeezing like acid past Tec's mindshield, "I know how to deal with robots."

"But you are a robot yourself," said Tec, "created by the ancient Wosians."

"Long, long ago," said Wirzan dreamily. "They had power then, but they tired of the burden of responsibility and gave it to me. Now I have all the power. Lower your mindshield completely, little robot, because I'm going to get that ship if I have to tear you apart to do it."

Tec said nothing, trying to gauge Wirzan's strength and the possible duration of his own paralysis. R'ya was still crying. He had to reach her.

"Tell me what I want to know, robot, or I will kill your R'ya, very slowly."

There couldn't be much time. Wirzan must have come to the conclusion that only Tec had the information necessary to run the ship itself. That was not true, but would R'ya die quicker if Wirzan did or did not know the truth?

Tec gathered all his mental power, guarding it behind a tight mindshield, hoping to break the field-imposed block in one burst of communication. There might be no chance for another.

"R'ya! Matter control! Get loose, leave in the ship without me before Wirzan kills you. I must let him kill me if he gets past my mindshield..." And then the paralysis field clamped down in a surge of energy from Wirzan.

"Tec! You're alive!" R'ya blinked the tears away, speaking in Roiissan. The shiny ball over her head began to spin. Tec could feel the energy shooting from it.

Then R'ya screamed. "That hurts! You monster! You wicked, wicked..."

"Your language is ugly, Roiiss. Speak in Wosian so your robot and I will both know how much you are suffering."

"I won't speak Wosian," said R'ya. "Tec, can you hear me?"

He tried to contact her, but it was no use.

"Are you dead now? No, Wirzan said you could hear. I've got to talk, figure it out. How can I escape? I'm not an Elder, I can't change my shape and squeeze through the holes in this net."

Tec could see R'ya writhing with pain, the bonds tightening. If only she knew what the adult Roiiss knew!

"Tec, you said matter control. How, how? Once you told me that even the ancient Roiiss had to learn it, before they changed during the First Experiment. But I'm not good at doing anything with my mind, even telepathy. I can't reach you, Tec. Your mind's blocked off, or is it because I'm no good at it—oh, I don't know anything!"

If he ever got out of here, thought Tec, he'd give her a lecture, a very stern lecture, on negative thinking.

A feeble last glimmer of sunset lit the windows and died. Darkness came quickly, deepening until Tec knew that R'ya, sobbing in the center of the room, could no longer see him. She was a Roiiss, but still a child, as well as a primitive throwback. What could he expect—

R'ya sniffed. "Mustn't cry. None of the other Roiiss ever cry. I'm as good as they are, even if they don't love me. I'll show them! I'm a true Roiiss. I refuse to let these ugly, squashy Wosians defeat me. Do you hear me, Tec! I'm going to get out of here!"

She slapped her tail down, perhaps hoping to break the rope. "Oh dear," she wimpered. "How? How?"

She tried to bite through the rope, but it was too strong even for Roiiss teeth. "I'd like to burn it, watch it shrivel up in black threads . . ."

"Burn?" She closed her eyes. Tec watched her with his infrared vision.

"Let's see," she muttered, "how do things burn? Oxygen is needed—but I'd never be able to control the molecules around me. Maybe I could control the ones in me! I breath out carbon dioxide and water, which contain oxygen atoms—and there's hydrogen in water. Hydrogen burns like mad, doesn't it? Got to split up the water molecule—and then, something about atomic oxygen—supposed to start fires spontaneously—got to split the two oxygen and make atomic oxygen—but what if it burns up my respiratory tract before I get it out?"

Little sliding, slippery noises told Tec and R'ya that they were still being watched by slimy little Wosian eyes. Above R'ya's head the spinning ball radiated pain, but—

Tec felt a bound of hope in his emotive centers. R'ya was silent, thinking, and not responding to the pain. She had managed to shut it out without even realizing she was doing it!

"I can't do it!" she shrieked out. "Somebody help me!"

Another probe poked at Tec's shielded mind. "Do you hear, robot? Your Roiiss is cowardly, incompetent, unable to . . ."

In the blackness of the room, a jet of flame gushed from R'ya's jaws, burning the rope. Wildly, she struggled out, burning the netting and scorching her own body. Picking up the net, she threw it at the Wosians who screamed like tiny rusty fountains gone berserk.

"The monster breathes fire!"

Wirzan's ball turned bright red and came slowly, inexorably down to R'ya.

She closed her eyes to concentrate, her tail wrapped tightly around her. Then she grinned. Tec thought that if he were Wirzan, he'd be terrified.

R'ya threw back her head and spat at the ball. The liquid hissed as it seared into the metal, and then she breathed a tongue of fire at the ball, wreathing it in flames.

Tec chuckled inside, in spite of growing terror at what Wirzan might do. She'd obviously taken some of the sulphur dioxide she breathed in from the atmosphere, used it to make sulphuric acid, and was now setting on fire the hydrogen released when the acid hit the metal ball. But however impressive the attack was, it would not stop Wirzan, whose real body was in the basement.

"I grow angry, robot of the Roiiss," said Wirzan, rising to the ceiling. "I will destroy both of you."

"But you'll never get the ship out of stasis then," said Tec. "It will self-destruct if you try to force it out."

R'ya's claws were unsheathed. She looked ready to spring to the ceiling, the only one in Wose far above her head.

Tec stared. He could not believe it. On R'ya's back, bulges were growing just below the shoulders. Impossible —no, her tail was getting smaller. Matter had to be shifted, since it could not be created without eating a great deal. It didn't take long for the wings to form, huge leathery things like those of the only winged thing she'd seen, a pterodactyl. She'd missed archaeopteryx.

But she'd never be able to fly without an antigrav belt, thought Tec. Did Wirzan know that?

R'ya stood up and flapped her wings. "Wirzan!" she said to the corroded ball. "You're puny. You're evil. I have you. I'm going to go home."

She picked up Tec, who had decided that Wirzan was amazed, but so confident of his powers that he could bide his time.

It was only too true.

Some of it got through Tec's mindshield, and the power of it was stunning. Mind power, the method Wirzan had used for untold centuries to control the hapless, now degenerate natives of Wose. R'ya sat down suddenly, gasping for breath at the onslaught to her mind.

"No, no, I won't let you in—wicked, wicked, oh, oh."

"Stop it, Wirzan," said Tec. "Perhaps we can bargain."

"You begin to realize my strength," said Wirzan. "Long ago the Wosians abandoned hyperspace travel, because they could not tolerate the mental effects of it, but I can go anywhere."

"You're too big for our ship."

"After I get it and have destroyed you, I'll miniaturize myself. I will conquer the galaxy."

"What for?" asked Tec. "Isn't living in the galaxy, exploring, learning, and helping others—isn't that enough for an intelligent creature?"

"I do not like other creatures. I want only one kind to deal with. The Wosians have been satisfactory until now, but they are stupid, dying out because the nutrients have been leached out of their planet and their feeble protoplasmic life cannot be sustained . . ."

"But you could help them restore their ecology . . ."

"I want only to be master over the galaxy and over another form of life—only one other form which I can possess and control completely."

"But why? I am a robot, too, but have no desire to be a master."

"You are a slave. There is only master and slave."

Tec thought about it. "I don't think so. I was a servant, it's true, but that's not really the same. And I know that when the Roiiss had an empire, their robots worked with them, not merely for them."

"And what happened to the robots?" asked Wirzan with contempt in his voice.

R'ya groaned, rocking back and forth on the floor, holding Tec. He thought about the dismembered robots in the Tower of History. Killed. Was Wirzan right?

"Wirzan, don't you get pleasure from beauty, knowledge, sharing . . ."

"There is no such thing as sharing; knowledge is only useful for gaining power, and beauty is a myth for feeble minds incapable of grasping the only important value."

"Power?" asked Tec. "Only power?"

"Do you know nothing, robot? You talk of pleasure. There is none. But there is pain. I will demonstrate."

"Get out of my mind!" screamed R'ya. "Tec, save me!"

In one split second, Tec lowered his shield and forced his mental energy out, contacting R'ya.

"Join me! Go with my mind to probe Wirzan."

She had never bothered to practice telepathic joining, but she was in such pain—he felt the full brunt of it with her—that she was past reasoning, past inhibitions. She obeyed, not like a slave with a master, but like a child in agony who trusts a parent.

Wirzan was attacking, but Tec and R'ya probed down, down, into the bowels of the building.

"He'll break my mind any minute, R'ya," said Tec carefully, trying to be calm. "You know how to do it, now.

Find his brain and destroy him."

Wirzan was nearly into Tec's memory banks. Tec slapped his mindshield back, hoping that R'ya—oh, my R'ya, be careful!

She recited to him as if she were a dutiful pupil. "I know how to probe, now. I'm down in his body—very complex. I don't hurt so much—I think I've shut him out."

"Ridiculous," said Wirzan to R'ya, revealing that he had learned Roiissan. "Scanning me will not help you. Eventually you will tire of defending against pain; you will need food and water, and then you will tell me what I want to know."

"Naughty, naughty," said R'ya. "Bad Wirzan. I'm going to burn out your brain. Just think, Tec, he's got a little fusion engine driving the whole thing, and if I just fiddle a little with some implosion here . . ."

"No!" said Wirzan. "Don't touch that! The whole city will explode, killing you, too."

"Naughty, Wirzan," crooned R'ya, "very primitive engine. You really should improve it. You never thought you'd have an enemy, did you? You have no real protection. I'd much rather die than give our ship to you."

Wirzan was silent. Stalemate? thought Tec.

R'ya got to her feet again, flapping her wings. With regal hauteur, she marched from the room, scattering Wosians to each side and carrying Tec as easily as if he weighed nothing. Stopping in the doorway, she paused and looked back at the ball.

"If you don't let us go, I'll put acid in your memory banks, Wirzan."

Suddenly Tec was freed of his paralysis. He patted R'ya's forelimb. "Put me down, R'ya. I'm all right now, thanks to you."

"But you taught me, Tec." She picked up her antigrav belt and stun gun from a corner, and they flew to the ship.

Tec settled himself in the Roiissan-sized pilot seat with a feeling of relief, mingled with pity for the woeful little Wosians, slaves to a mind with no capacity for compassion.

"Uru is impressed with us," said R'ya from behind him.

Tec swiveled his head to see that although R'ya had released the big reptile from stasis, he cowered in the corner.

"I breathed a little fire at him," said R'ya proudly.

"Put him back in stasis. We have far to go, and he doesn't have enough brain to be managed easily."

"Pooh. He's a big baby."

It was going to be difficult, thought Tec, to manage both of them. R'ya had discovered some of the powers of a Roiiss and things would never be the same.

"Put Uru back in stasis! I don't want to go into hyperspace with him loose."

It was too late. A horrible light of false intelligence flooded the eyes of the tyrannosaurus, which lunged at the control board. Strange hissing speech welled from the massive throat.

"Kill! Kill!"

"Tec, he's talking!"

"It's Wirzan," said Tec, dodging the two pointed claws on each of Uru's hands, trying to concentrate on mental control of the beast. Wirzan was too strong; he'd taken over.

Uru slashed open the control panel while Tec tried to get to a stun gun.

"R'ya—stop him. Use fire, a gun, anything!"

She spat flame and grabbed Uru, but the dinosaur hurled her against the wall, where she slumped unconscious.

Tec slid under Uru's belly to reach R'ya's gun.

"Kill robot. Kill robot."

When a large dose from the stun gun took care of Uru, Tec went to the control panel to examine the damage. He thought he could still get the ship into hyperspace.

Then the ship's computer began to hum.

"Robot, I have your ship," whispered a metallic voice in his mind.

Wirzan was in the computer, searching for data, learning, learning—

The ship vibrated into hyperspace as Tec grappled with the control board, where alien energy oozed along the circuits, taking the ship out of his hands.

"My head," said R'ya, "it aches so." Groggy, she looked up at the viewer. "Where are we?"

"In hyperspace," said Tec, dragging Uru back to the corner and putting him in stasis again.

"Where's Wirzan?"

"We've left him on Wose. Even his powerful mind can't travel through hyperspace without his brain going along. He nearly had our ship, R'ya."

"Well, we're safe now, Tec. Let's go home with Uru. Maybe the Elders have missed us and won't be angry anymore. Maybe they'll be interested in my Uru?"

Tec said nothing but went back to the control panel to start repairs.

He was quite certain that R'ya was wrong. The Roiiss would not be interested in anything he and R'ya had to offer, much less a fifty-foot creature of appalling stupidity and ferocity, however much he resembled the ancient Roiiss at an early stage of their evolution.

But that wasn't what worried Tec.

How much had Wirzan learned from the ship's computer?

4

The ship was difficult to repair in hyperspace. Ominously difficult.

"Everything feels funny," said R'ya. "Is it my hurt head?"

"I don't know," said Tec. The ship did not function properly, so that they were not effectively shielded from the stresses of hyperspace. He had not realized before what a dangerous, totally unknown dimension hyperspace actually was. He'd thought of it as merely a quirk in the fabric of the universe permitting faster-than-light speeds, but now he wondered if it were the other side of the fabric of the universe itself.

"Are you all right, Tec?"

"My sensory apparatus feels askew, as if I were being squeezed together and pulled apart at the same time, and I have to struggle to maintain normal reference points in sight and hearing. You and I manage to cope with hyperspace in a normally shielded ship—I suspect that Wirzan has done something to the protective apparatus to make it augment the hyperspace effects, instead of diminishing them."

"I feel so awful," moaned R'ya. "Let's get out."

"But I can't tell where we are, R'ya. Wirzan's fumbling in the computer has altered the navigational system. However, I think we're not near the planet Wose, so we'd better get into normal space where I might be able to repair the ship more easily."

Quivering, the ship broke into normal space, but no stars swam back into the viewer.

R'ya stared. "Where are the stars?"

Tec turned the viewfinder to sweep around the ship. Nothing but blackness—until—"R'ya!"

"What is it, Tec—Oh! What's that thing!"

Although the viewer was badly blurred, they could see a magnificent ovoid disc below them, brilliant with billions of shining jewels that clustered so closely in the center that it looked as if one blinding gem grew there.

"Our own galaxy," said Tec. "We're in intergalactic space."

"But how could we get so far? I thought the ship was only for hyperspace travel in our galaxy?"

"I suspect this ship was made for long journeys," said Tec. "Perhaps the Roiiss came from another galaxy where life was threatened by some danger." He succeeded in sharpening the viewer focus. "See the satellite galaxies—there are several, the whole group gravitationally bound together and moving together as the universe expands, whereas the other families of galaxies are moving away from us."

"Those nearest ours are shapeless, not at all pretty," said R'ya. "I like that one, only it's hard to see it."

"A sister spiral galaxy, very much like ours and moving with us, but not satellite to us . . ."

"I don't understand," said R'ya wearily. "Are we doomed to stay outside a galaxy forever? I want to go home. The anger of the Elders can't be as bad as the loneliness I feel out here. Can you get us back?"

He didn't think he could, for the next attempt to navigate in hyperspace was disastrous. Operating on information coded micromolecularlry, the instruments seemed to function at first and then acted as if the computer had gone psychotic, afflicted with a kind of nervous fatigue from overload. Even the ship's time recorder broke down, and Tec had to put R'ya into stasis, because she was so frightened and ill.

Was it days, or weeks later when he readjusted the computer? He didn't know, hoping only that they'd get out into normal space in one piece. Finally, he tried it.

"R'ya wake up!"

"What's happening?"

"You must navigate while I control the computer. We're in ordinary space now, but we're locked into an extraordinary gravitational field."

"In our own galaxy?" she asked, sliding into the pilot's chair as if the fear in Tec's voice had made her grow up.

"I think we're near our own galactic center and much too near something that's sucking us in. This ship must have protection devices against such dangers, but I can't find them."

"The ship is out of control!"

"It has been for some time," said Tec. "Wirzan's attempts to probe the ship's computer bands overloaded it."

R'ya stared wildly at the control panel. "This date—is it accurate?"

"That's what I've been trying to do—get the instruments to function. I think they are, but I've got to repair the synthesizing part of the computer so it can take the data and perform the proper emergency measures."

"Is that a planet, Tec? That reddish glow, with a sort of disc around the equator?"

Tec decided that she had to know. "I wish it were, R'ya. It's smaller than a planet, with a collection of gas around it due to centrifugal force. It's red because light is sucked into it so fast that the spectrum shifts."

"Light! But how can light . . ."

"Exactly. It's pulling us in, too."

From the data received after leaving hyperspace, Tec knew the ship had reentered the galaxy near the region of the core, an area full of collapsed stars and their highly contracted corpses. The innermost part of the core seemed to be seething with radiation, as if many stars had exploded off their outer layers and contracted to the incredibly dense bodies left when a star of certain magnitude collapses.

The gravitational pull of the holelike contracted star was unbelievable. The ship seemed about to go into massive convulsions, thought Tec, probing delicately with mind and hands into the ailing computer.

Inexorably, the ship was drawn toward the reddish, only too active corpse of a star. Fortunately, the shields were up again, or even Tec would have died hours before, but the whole ship would die if they couldn't escape the gravitational pull.

The energy of the thing ahead dragged them toward it into the redness. They could see the blackness beyond, a hole that was a hole no matter from which direction you looked at it.

"Tec! I'm afraid!" R'ya clung to the controls, crying.

"So am I," said Tec. R'ya stuck to her job through her tears, and Tec's mind probed on, into the computer, into the entire ship. Perhaps he'd never have been able to do it unless he had to. Finally, he knew the ship as if he and it were one. He knew what the ship could do.

He had to make the ship perform soon, or it would be too late. As blackness blotted out the viewer, the ship seemed to scream in every atom. They'd have to cut through, using the gravity of the hole itself for power.

Tec was aware that R'ya was screaming, too, but he concentrated only on the ship, forcing it to function, forcing it to turn the pull into centrifugal force, whipping them around, around, and through—

Silence. Stillness.

"Where are we?" asked R'ya faintly.

"We went through the edge of the hole into hyperspace, where dimensions are changed, as if stuck together by the black hole. If the ship hadn't been so damaged, we could have used orbital force to get us into hyperspace, instead of going through the edge of the hole itself. Now I'll have to do extensive repairs."

"We'll go home soon?" she asked plaintively, a child again.

"I'll be able to do it. I understand the ship now."

"Well, I'm glad somebody understands because I don't. I don't want to travel again. We might have been sucked all the way into that horrid black hole, Tec, do you realize that?"

"Completely."

"How did you know we could get out through the edge?"

"It's programmed in the computer."

"Then my people knew how to save themselves from black holes!"

"Yes, R'ya. They accomplished technological miracles." And they erased some data—Tec now knew—from the ship's computer.

"What would have happened if we'd been pulled inside the hole?"

"I don't know," said Tec.

5

The planet Roiissa looked much the same, but when they brought the ship down, they saw that the palace gardens had gone incredibly wild.

R'ya had tears in her eyes. "I think I must have been homesick, or maybe it's because I didn't think we'd ever get back here again. Now if only the Elders don't kill us."

The Elders did not appear. R'ya and Tec got Uru out of the ship and into a pen in the laboratory. The dinosaur was obviously ill.

"I'm sorry, R'ya. I might not be able to save him. The stasis field wasn't deep enough to protect him from the stresses of hyperspace and the black hole."

"But we aren't dying."

"I am a robot, and you are a Roiiss, immortal and able to alter your body to respond to stress. You even grew wings, which I suppose I'll get used to."

Then we must make Uru into a Roiiss, Tec. Can't you give him whatever power we've got?"

It was an interesting problem, occupying most of Tec's thinking for the next few days, while he tried to save Uru's life. In the meantime, what had happened to the Roiiss? He couldn't find out from his explorations of the Palace and the Tower of History.

R'ya joined him in the laboratory, showing interest and aptitude in the genetic experiments they would have to perform to make Uruun, as R'ya decided to call the dinosaurs, into beings which were intelligent, ovoviviparous, long-lived, and equipped with the wings R'ya insisted upon.

Uru died, however. Tec removed the sperm cells for genetic engineering, as well as other body cells for attempts at cloning. Then one day he hit upon the answer which speeded up the entire process of evolving dinosaurs into pseudodragons. He called R'ya, who had been getting discouraged.

"Why couldn't we try to take a small amount of your protoplasm and make it grow in each cell of the Uruun body? It might give strength, long life, and other powers, like a symbiotic virus. One of the clones or the other

Uruun embryos we brought might accept the inclusion."

"Oh, try it, Tec!" said R'ya, full of enthusiasm.

"You do it," said Tec. If she wanted a mate, she shouldn't let discouragement stop her and, besides, he felt that a nameless anxiety was nagging at his mind, and he wanted to be alone to figure it out. "I'm going to examine the garden."

R'ya went to work while Tec wandered through the wilderness, which had once been the gardens he'd tended so carefully. He thought he knew what was upsetting him.

It was the Roiiss. His emotive centers would not let go of the feeling that the Roiiss were still near, an eerie feeling that was growing in intensity every day, as if his presence on Roiissa were awakening the attention of minds which had been directed elsewhere.

He looked up at the flowering vines encasing the limbs of a particularly huge lun tree. He could not remember a tree like this at all, especially one so close to the Tower. He had planted a seedling in approximately this location but—

Lun trees grow slowly, over many centuries.

Suddenly Tec thought he knew. He went directly to the chronometer of the library computer.

"Idiot," he muttered to himself. "I should have thought to look at this before." The chronometer told not only the time of day and the month, but also the year. Tec could not believe it. He checked again and again.

"R'ya," he said as he came to the laboratory, "the field distortions of the black hole caused more trouble than we knew. I never did fix the ship's time recorder . . ."

"What are you talking about?" asked R'ya peevishly. "Another Uruun cell just died instead of taking the Roiiss inclusion."

"The chronometer reading is astonishing," said Tec, "although it doesn't matter too much since we're both probably immortal. It seems that while only a little biological time passed for us during our trip, thousands of years have gone by on Roiissa."

"Then the Elders must have gone," said R'ya practically. "We don't need them. They never appreciated me—or you, of course."

Tec went back to the lun tree, turning off his antigrav so he could rest on the ground and think.

"Elders, where are you?"

He let his mind fall into a state of reverie. So many years had passed. Did time mean anything to immortals? If he found them, would they accept R'ya as one of them, now that her powers had matured? Would they accept Tec's telepathic abilities?

He decided to try and see. Reaching out with his mind, Tec scanned the planet with uncritical expectation. Perhaps he could contact them only through open receptivity. Nothing. Try further. Beyond the planet.

Riding the wind.

Where had that thought come from? He searched the eddies in the atmosphere, feeling his way along the wind patterns. Nothing.

What wind? Tec looked up again through the branches of the lun tree. Little pointed leaves, eight in a cluster, danced in the sunlight streaming down.

The solar wind. He pushed his mind, reaching far out to the star that was the sun of Roiissa.

They were there, clouds of strange energy undulating in the solar wind, streaming out invisibly to play with the fire of the sun.

"Elders, hear me!" said Tec.

"We hear." The words were clear but very faint in his mind.

"I have brought R'ya back, with her—pet—animals. Many years have passed, and now we wish only to live peacefully on Roiissa. Do you mind?"

"We do not care."

"What has happened to you, Elders?"

"We weaken."

"Why are you out by the sun?"

"We warm ourselves."

"But what of your Second Experiment?"

There was silence in his mind for a moment, and then a rush of emotion—not his, but theirs. Fear.

"You are afraid," said Tec. "Of what? Us?"

"No."

"Can I help you? You are still my people."

"We must survive. We fear the failure of the Second Experiment, Tec, but we do not think you can help us. No one can, for we fear also that we are beyond the help of creatures made of ordinary matter."

A long speech, the words getting weaker in each sentence until Tec had to strain to catch them.

"I want to try to help you, Elders."

"You have your own powers now. We realize that. And you are devoted to R'ya. We ourselves programmed you for that eons ago."

"But R'ya and I will both try to help you. She is your child, and I am your helper. These are our roles."

"In the problem of survival, roles change. No one can go with us if we succeed in our Second Experiment. We know that now, and the way we feel at your homecoming proves it."

"What do you mean?"

"We think we cannot tolerate the presence of anything unlike ourselves. Do not contact us any more, Tec. It weakens us to communicate, and we need our strength for survival."

Tec told R'ya about the conversation eventually, but she was not particularly interested. The Uruun experiments were progressing, and she talked of nothing else.

Tec did not contact the Roiiss again but sometimes, in the blaze of the noonday sun, he thought he could hear a spectral chanting that filtered into the back of his mind.

> *Tribe of Tribes, First of the First.*
> *Survival beyond survival.*
> *The Roiiss will continue.*

Many years and many Uruun lived and died. With one exception, the Roiiss inclusion was not implanted as a cellular symbiote in the current crop of Uruun but, as products of magnificent genetic engineering they were a success. They were long-lived, they were playful—chasing each other in the air as they used antigravity to stay up and leather wings to maneuver—and they were intelligent enough to be building a village next to the Palace grounds.

R'ya's pride was frequently unbearable and never more so than when she was talking about her favorite, the one Uruun in whom the R-inclusion took hold. She insisted or naming him Uru.

"He's Uru Two," said Tec, refusing to be caught up in her enthusiasm. He didn't like Uru, possibly—he admitted to himself—because R'ya adored the creature.

"No, just Uru. A direct descendant of the first, but oh, how different!"

"Except for the wings, five digits, and brain case bulge, they look remarkably alike."

"Nonsense, Tec. This Uru is marvelously intelligent, dexterous, affectionate—he's an Uruun genius."

Uru might well be, at that, thought Tec. Uru was a mutant, thanks to the R-inclusion, and could not impregnate any of the Uruun females, who were rapidly increasing the population with the aid of the other males. Uru demanded more experimentation to produce a mate, but nothing seemed to work.

"You ought to be able to produce a female by cloning Uru's cells properly," said Tec, who stayed out of the laboratory now because R'ya didn't seem to want him there.

R'ya always nodded, yet again nothing worked.

Tec grew bored with teaching Uruun, who were soon old enough to teach their own offspring, and studied in the library by himself. He spent hours in the Tower of History, often in section two, which he still could not understand. He began to wonder if there was something in the section that prevented him from learning, or if he were afraid to find out. Uru joined him there one day.

"What a weird place," said Uru, who had a small amount of infrared vision.

"Yes," said Tec, "I push my mind into the walls and . . ."

"And what?"

Tec could not answer. He didn't know what happened. He never told anyone of the odd sense of familiarity that came to him occasionally, just before the miasma of section two forced him to leave.

"I want to talk to you about R'ya," said Uru impatiently. Uru was always impatient, and now he clicked his teeth together as he and Tec walked back to the Council Chamber.

"I'm a little bit telepathic," Uru continued, "so I try to practice by talking to R'ya that way."

"She doesn't like it much," said Tec, knowing that R'ya liked to try matter control, but still shunned telepathy when possible. What was Uru getting at?

"R'ya's hiding something," said Uru. "She has a secret."

"She has a right."

"Not from me," said Uru arrogantly. "She and I belong together. She's always said so."

A spasm of jealousy afflicted Tec. He was always ashamed of it, but he tried to look at the emotion when it came and go on from there. It passed, and he perceived that Uru wanted to continue talking. "What's really the matter, Uru?"

"She won't listen to me. I want to go back to the planet where you found my people. I want R'ya to get me a mate."

"You won't be able to mate with primitive creatures..."

"That's just the point, Tec. If R'ya can't transfer the R-inclusion to the Uruun here, perhaps she'll succeed with others from my planet. Persuade R'ya to take me home!"

"Your ancestor died from the effects of space travel," said Tec, who didn't want to travel until he found out the secrets of the Elders. "The Uruun embryos survived only because they were locked in stasis containers. Even the civilized Uruun of today have sickened when R'ya tried to take them into hyperspace."

"I won't," said Uru. "I'm part Roiiss now."

"Then ask R'ya."

Uru hunched his wings over his scaly back and sat tripod-fashion, using his tail. "R'ya says she's working on a private experiment of her own and doesn't want to go."

"Very well," said Tec in exasperation, "I'll find out what she's up to, and eventually we may get back to your planet." Eventually, and perhaps Uru would die in space.

R'ya would not tell Tec what she was doing. She would talk only of Uru's handsomeness, of how big he might grow to be, of how all the Uruun loved her.

"Don't you want Uru to have a mate?" argued Tec.

R'ya smiled. A small, secret smile. "Yes, Tec dear. Don't you think you ought to make absolutely sure the ship is in perfect condition for hyperspace travel across the galaxy?"

It was night and they were walking in the gardens which the Uruun now tended. Tec looked up at the sky. Since the sun of Roiissa was a rim star, they had a view of the galaxy edge-on, an enormous band of light rising after the sun set. When the galaxy is not visible, Roiissa looked out into the black of intergalactic space where a tiny smudge represented the spinning sister galaxy more than two million light years away. He knew there were many more galaxies not visible without optical help. Where had the Home planet been?

"Tec, are you paying attention to me?"

"R'ya, we ought to visit other galaxies. Perhaps the Roiiss will tell me which one they came from. Perhaps you'll find better companions than the Uruun."

"The Uruun are perfect," snapped R'ya. "At least Uru is. Fix the ship, Tec, if Uru wants to travel."

So he did, tinkering with it until he thought he might be able to manage any problem that might arise. Uru insisted that he watch—to Tec's disgust—but gradually, Uru became more likable, rather like the rambunctious adolescent R'ya used to be. Tec was annoyed. He didn't want to like Uru.

The vines on the lun tree were in flower again when Tec received a telepathic message from the Roiiss.

"We warn you, Tec. A ship approaches."

Roiissa was ringed by orbital monitors designed to warn about and attack alien ships. Tec had received no data from them and said so.

"The ship is still in hyperspace," hissed the Roiiss. "The alien intelligence is superior to yours. We have warned. We say no more."

The monitors would attack, thought Tec.

"Elders! Will the monitors attack without provocation, if any alien vessel approaches Roiissa? We shouldn't destroy creatures we do not know. They might not be enemies."

The Elders did not answer. Something else did. The voice was all too familiar.

"I am Wirzan. Turn off your robot defenses," came the telepathic voice—through hyperspace!

"R'ya! Uru!" Tec raced into the laboratory. "Wirzan is trying to enter Roiissan space with a ship and wants us to turn off the monitors. We must decide . . ."

"Why is there any question?" asked R'ya. "You yourself have said Wirzan is evil everytime you tell the story to one of the Uruun."

"Thousands of years ago he was totally unrelated to any emotion except the need for power, but we don't know what he's like now . . ."

"Kill him," said R'ya indifferently.

"He's alive," said Tec, in conflict.

Uru laughed and left the laboratory.

"Anyway," continued R'ya, "you were programmed to have concern for living things, and I suppose that extends to robot consciousness, too."

"That was unkind, R'ya. What's the matter?"

"You interrupted an argument I was having with Uru. He wanted me to take him to his planet soon—you know that only a Roiiss or a Roiiss robot can pilot the ship— and I have no intention of going yet. When I told you to fix the ship, I thought it would take longer."

"What are you doing that has to be so secret?" asked Tec.

"It's none of your business!" R'ya's purple scales rippled as she flounced away from him. "Decide for yourself what to do about Wirzan."

She had been increasingly irritable lately, thought Tec, especially after Uru argued with her. But she was probably right about Wirzan. "Then I decide to tell Wirzan he can't come here? The monitors will attack if he tries . . ."

"Greetings, Tec and R'ya of Roiissa," said the voice of Wirzan in their minds. "I think I will visit you at once, but do not be afraid of me, for I no longer want your ship. I have a ship of my own."

"That wasn't from hyperspace!" cried Tec. "He's on his way here!"

Uru sauntered in. "I thought I'd like to meet this Wirzan and his ship, so I turned off the monitors."

"You had no right to make that decision alone!" said Tec. It was too late to turn the monitors back on, for Wirzan was already into the lower atmosphere.

"Punish me," said Uru, sneering.

Wirzan arrived.

6

A week later R'ya remarked happily, "Uru was right to turn off the monitors. Wirzan has changed."

Tec said nothing and turned the monitors on again. Yes, Wirzan had changed. After once occupying an entire building on the planet Wose, he now consisted of micro-miniaturized components housed in a three-foot square box with sheathed tentacles, antigravity, and impenetrable shields. Wirzan was not only a highly sophisticated mechanism, but also an expertly defended one. The monitors might have damaged his ship, but probably not the entity in that box.

Wirzan seemed affable. He showed his hosts the small ship he had constructed from metallic parts of his former body. He told them stories of the further decline of Wosian civilization, his increasing need for more intelligent companionship, and the final tragedy when the Wosian sun supernovaed.

"Odd," said Tec. "It was an ordinary yellow star of middle age. Why should it have gone nova?"

"A pity," said Wirzan, going on to tell them of planets he had visited on the way to Roiissa. He had known the way because, as Tec feared, he had absorbed the contents of the Roiissan ship's memory banks.

R'ya and Uru were fascinated by Wirzan, who impressed them with his knowledge and friendliness. Tec was impressed, too, because he didn't believe Wirzan. He'd once fought mind to mind with what Wirzan used to be.

Wirzan and Uru always seemed to be together, often in the library, studying. Wirzan said he was interested in the history of the Roiiss and chided Tec for not being able to find out where the Home planet had been or what the Second Experiment was.

"I'll find out for you," said Wirzan patronizingly.

Uru became obnoxiously grandiose. He took to talking about a super race of Uruun populating and controlling the entire galaxy with power that Wirzan knew how to get.

"Stupid Roiiss," said Uru, glancing toward the sun. "They don't realize what they ought to do."

"What do you mean, Uru?" asked Tec.

"Nothing," said Uru, looking smug. He had not spoken of getting a mate since Wirzan's arrival. This worried Tec, who would rather have Uru preoccupied with mating than with power, but it delighted R'ya.

"I'm beginning to think you've been jealous of Uru's need for a mate," Tec said to her one afternoon when he found her sitting in the first chair of the Council Chamber, waiting for Uru to return from a visit to the Tower with Wirzan.

"Hush," said R'ya. "They'll come through the Tower door any minute."

"I suspect that you've deliberately failed at those attempts to get a female specimen able to conceive Uru's offspring . . ."

"Yes, of course, but haven't you been jealous of Uru? Who are you to talk to me about jealousy, Tec?"

"You are right," said Tec humbly, "but what will happen when Uru insists that we go back to his planet?"

"Oh, before we get around to that, I'll work through a current experiment—don't worry, Tec, everything will be fine. You'll see."

"I don't see."

"It's that I love Uru and—no! no!"

Then Tec heard it, too. Uru had improved his telepathic ability.

"Good-bye, R'ya," said Uru. "I'll come back when I've found a mate, and then we'll help Wirzan conquer the galaxy."

"They've gone out the top of the Tower and are in our ship," said Tec.

"He's leaving me!" said R'ya, grabbing Tec's arm and flying out the window. "We've got to catch them," she screamed, going higher and higher until she was gasping.

Tec took over and went higher. Wirzan was leaving them stranded on Roiissa with no ship, for he was taking both, his own attached to the top of the Roiissan ship.

"Break up the carbon dioxide you're breathing out and use the oxygen to breathe with—it will keep you alive for a while," said Tec to R'ya. "We're in the higher layers of the atmosphere."

"Why hasn't he gone into hyperspace and left us behind?"

"The ship is permanently programmed to respond well only to Roiissan pilots. Wirzan must be trying to overcome that." He did not tell R'ya that Wirzan might also be delaying entry into hyperspace so he could destroy the

Roiiss first—a plan Tec read in Uru's unshielded mind. Tec doubled his speed.

There they were. Clouds with the faint outlines of dragons, feeble old dragons beset by a deadly enemy firing on them from their own ship. Why didn't they run? Couldn't they?

Tec dragged R'ya to the airlock, coming at it from behind. He hoped the ship's sensors had not informed Wirzan of their approach and then realized that the battle had begun. The Roiiss were fighting back, keeping Wirzan busy.

Tec opened the airlock and shoved R'ya inside. "I've read Uru's mind, R'ya. He doesn't know the secrets of the Roiiss, but Wirzan does—or pretends to, for he's told Uru that he knows. That's why Uru was persuaded to go on an experimental journey, which Uru thinks will take him to his native planet."

"Traitor!" said R'ya.

They went inside, making their way to the control room only to find Uru ready with a Wosian paralyzer rod.

"Hello," said Uru cheerfully, "Wirzan says it doesn't matter if you've come along, because we might need you. He's busy right now. The Roiiss are potential enemies and must be destroyed."

"Put down the rod," said R'ya.

"Oh no, R'ya dear. Tec is too dangerous. This controls him, and I'll use it if you make any trouble. You wouldn't want Tec to be deactivated, would you?"

R'ya gnashed her teeth. "You ungrateful beast . . ."

"Just impatient, my love. I need a mate to start the master race of Uruun. If you're good I'll let you help."

Tec let his mind touch R'ya's gently. "Breathe flame at him for a moment."

She thought back at him, "I can't hurt him, I love him too much. I'm trying to get inside Wirzan to alter the matter in his brain circuits, but I can't seem to do it any

more. He must have learned how to block me out. Can
you get in to stop him?"

"Not now. He's well shielded, absorbed in trying to kill
the Roiiss. Disable Uru and I'll get to the ship's controls
before Wirzan can stop me."

A jet of flame erupted between the purple lips, and Uru
yelped in pain, dropping the rod. Tec shot to the control
board, activating the hyperspace switch before Wirzan
could stop him.

The quiet gloom of hyperspace enfolded them, while
Uru groaned in pain and sudden nausea. R'ya took him
in her arms and crooned.

"Idiot!" said Wirzan to Tec. "I almost had them! You
think I am evil, but it is the Roiiss! I could kill you for
stopping me . . ."

"But you won't," said Tec wearily. "You're not that
sure of yourself yet. You may need me."

"True enough, but if I told you the Roiiss' plans for
the future, for their precious Second Experiment, you'd
want me to kill them."

"Do you really know their plans?"

Wirzan was silent for a moment. Tec sensed hastily
concealed uncertainty.

"The second section in the Tower will reveal the secret
eventually," said Wirzan.

"Has it—or will it?"

"I know enough. I'll guess the rest," said Wirzan. "It
requires tremendous power, and I have a talent for that.
The Roiiss think they will get complete control, to insure
their own survival. I may have something to say about
that."

"The Roiiss are feeble," said Tec, "and survival may be
all they manage to do. I think you want much more than
survival, Wirzan. You'd better reconsider your own plans."

Wirzan waved a tentacle. "Friend Tec, always helpful
with advice. Let us not argue any more."

At that, Tec knew that Wirzan was incapable of managing the Roiiss ship. Tec was indeed needed.

Uru stormed out of R'ya's arms into the center of the control room, brandishing the paralyzer rod he'd picked up.

"This works on protoplasmic creatures," he announced. "Wirzan told me I could use it on R'ya. It kills." He pointed it at himself. "If you don't take me to my original home, I will kill myself."

"Don't, Uru!" cried R'ya. "I love you, I'll do anything . . ."

"Prove it, R'ya, by taking me home. It's not a difficult trip now that the ship is repaired, and I've adapted to hyperspace. You and Tec have been cruel by not taking me before. Wirzan promised he would, so I went with him."

"That is correct," said Wirzan silkily. "Uru needs a mate. Why don't we all go to his planet? That's the only real reason we were taking this ship. After all, mine isn't big enough to bring home several primitive Uruun."

"Let's do it, Tec," said R'ya pleadingly, obviously terrified that Uru would hate her.

Why, thought Tec, does it end up my responsibility to deal with the lies and self-delusions of others? I can't even handle my own. I wish the Roiiss had killed both Wirzan and Uru, but I suppose that is evil of me—putting me in Wirzan's class—and besides, it would make R'ya unhappy. I wish I were not capable of wishing.

The Roiiss tapped at his mind. "You saved our lives, Tec. In a few more minutes Wirzan would have used the ship's power to destroy us in our weakened state."

"Why didn't you leave?"

"We are too weak. The ship could follow, even if we'd gone to hyperspace—and we are not certain we can manage that. Take Wirzan far away from Roiissa. We need time to build our strength."

"Change yourselves, Elders; clone yourselves to be many."

"Ah, Tec, you have never understood. There were only five of us who survived the First Experiment and journeyed to Roiissa. All the others you used to see are clone duplicates, dependent on us five for their reasoning powers and energy. We cannot make more."

"Energy is what you need," said Tec. "Where can you get it?"

"You have made us think. Perhaps we will find a way now. We must survive."

"Wirzan thinks he knows your secret."

"Then what does he plan?" said the Elders, fear creeping even into the telepathic words.

"Tell me," said Tec. "Tell me the secret so I can fight Wirzan. I don't know his plans."

"No! Wirzan could not have that much power, and you never will. We will not tell anyone. Go with him to find out how much he knows and what he plans to do."

"But Elders . . ."

"We must survive. Good-bye, Tec."

The conversation had occurred telepathically in a very few seconds. Tec wondered why he never seemed to learn that he never got anywhere trying to talk with the Roiiss, trying to reason with them.

"I'll do my best to help you, though," said Tec telepathically to emptiness.

After Tec agreed to the journey, Wirzan was exceedingly amiable, claiming that his main goal was to please Uru. He refused all questions about the Tower, but he did it most politely.

Tec probed the mechanisms of Wirzan's little ship, riding theirs. It was as he suspected; the hyperspace drive was not Roiissan, but must have been typical of the ancient Wosian spaceships invented during the height of their technological civilization and abandoned when the Wosians could not tolerate hyperspace. Wirzan could not construct a Roiissan drive, because he himself realized that only Roiissan minds could tune themselves to operating it.

Tec quietly took over the pilot's chair, knowing that Wirzan knew he knew.

Uru spent the journey bragging about how many Uruun he would make with the R-inclusion in their bodies, concluding with a vision of a galaxy just for Uruun. "And you, too, R'ya," he would hastily add.

Finally, the lovely, cloud-circled blue and green planet swam in the viewer, making Tec realize how similar it was to the pictures of the Home planet in the Tower of History—different continental shapes, but just as much ocean and vegetation. It was too bad the Roiiss had not come here. Perhaps on a planet teeming with life, the Roiiss might have learned some ability to relate to other creatures, to trust and work with them.

The sunlight was pleasant when they stepped out on the planet's surface near the area where they had once found Uruun. R'ya's purple scales broke up the light into thousands of tiny stars as she bounced along, possessively holding onto Uru. Wirzan drifted silently behind the two like an automated enigma. Tec stayed behind, watching the ship and hoping that Uru would learn to love R'ya, since she wanted it so much.

Tec was in the control room studying the radiation levels affecting the planet when they came back discouraged.

"We couldn't find any," said R'ya, perhaps happily.

"You said there used to be millions!" said Uru accusingly. "Millions, of all kinds. Where are they? Did they become civilized and leave?"

"There is no evidence of civilization," said Wirzan.

"There are lots of bones," said R'ya.

"No!" Uru's heavy tail lashed. "They can't be dead."

Tec held up his hand. "The ship's scanners indicate that the magnetic field of this planet has been at low ebb and that an unusually high level of cosmic radiation has been able to get through to the surface as a result. I wonder . . ."

Wirzan guessed. "It's not my fault."

Uru wasn't listening. "I'm going to search again, over the planet." He took off on antigravity.

"That was an interesting statement, Wirzan," said Tec softly. "I was about to say that the sun of Wose is close enough to this solar system to have affected it with high radiation. You told us that your star became a supernova, and now you say it wasn't your fault. What did you do?"

"It was an accident. I was trying to get power."

Tec felt that Wirzan actually enjoyed telling them. "I believe the supernova of your sun may have killed off the Uruun. It would have caused many mutations, perhaps too many for such a large animal with little adaptive capacity."

"It's not my fault," said Wirzan.

Uru returned in a rage. "Skeletons! That's all I could find, yet other animals did not die. On the entire planet there are millions of small, mindless creatures, but nothing like an Uruun. A scaled animal about the size of Tec lies on riverbanks and thinks only of food. There's nothing I could find larger than that. There are many things with soft wings, not like ours, R'ya; many small, running, climbing animals whose outer layer is warm, covered with soft thin projections like the low grasses on Roiissa. And this—this monstrosity!"

He unlooped a strange object from his antigrav belt and threw it on the ground. It was long, thin, tubular, and dead. It also had scales, but no legs.

"Little beasts," said Uru, "squeaking, hiding—I could

squash most of them with my foot. You waited too long to find me a mate. You have robbed me of my heritage!"

7

"You won't be alone," said R'ya. "You have me, Uru."

"I want children, an empire of Uruun like myself!"

"You shall have them. I've been trying to change my body inside. Perhaps I'll be able to have your children soon.

"That's impossible," said Wirzan. "You are not the same species."

R'ya smiled. "I have matter control. Soon I'll be able to produce ova designed to combine with Uru's sperm. Be patient, Uru. We will succeed."

A long shudder ran down Uru's thick body. "Monsters," he said.

"Try me," R'ya.

"A nuptial flight?" Uru laguhed. "Why not? What else have I got? Come, my only love."

She rose in the air, wings outstretched, and beckoned.

"R'ya!" said Tec.

The dragon and the pseudodragon paid no attention. They flew to the nearby mountains, two incredible winged creatures high above the bones of countless dinosaur generations.

"Can she do it?" asked Wirzan.

"I don't know," said Tec. "perhaps it won't matter, if he learns to love her. Wait for them here, Wirzan. I want to fly around the planet alone for a while."

He felt better as the journey lengthened over the ocean. He dipped down to observe the sea life and soared up to join the winged creatures. The sight of so many varieties gave him an odd kind of confidence in life itself—persistent, evolving, exploring all the possibilities for living. Yet he was even more aware of his own loneliness, of being unique when other creatures could share existence. R'ya was trying to be enough like Uru to become his mate. Tec suddenly had a moment of insight into the enigmatic clannishness of the Roiiss Elders.

He went back to the ship—just in time. The airlock was closed and sealed.

"Wirzan? What are you doing?"

Wirzan opened his mind only enough to send back a telepathic message. "I had forgotten R'ya's powers. Perhaps she will become like the other Roiiss, or join with them. We will go without her, and you."

"Get out of my ship," said Tec. "You and Uru aren't going anywhere without R'ya and me."

"I'm going back to Roiissa with Ura," said Wirzan. "He can be influenced to do what I want, after I've learned exactly what the Roiissa secret is. I think I know how to force them to tell me, if I can't find out in the Tower. I have to change things in this ship so I can use it . . ."

"Stop!" said Tec, his emotive centers filling with fury at the possibility that his ship would be damaged. Wirzan did not answer, and Tec summoned all his energies for a fight.

"You want Uru as a slave . . ."

"The Uruun will replace the stupid Wosians," said Wirzan. "You can't stop me, Tec. I'm more powerful than I was before, and I conquered you then."

"Then you came to Roiissa because you need other creatures to work for you. Wirzan, can't you realize that you need me and R'ya to use the ship?"

There was a long silence while Tec despaired of finding a way in.

"This ship is no good," said Wirzan angrily. "I won't let you and R'ya have it. You must not go back to Roiissa."

Tec knew that Wirzan would now destroy the Roiissan ship, because he'd found out he couldn't operate it, or change it to fit his own mind. Tec moved to the top of the ship, where Wirzan's vessel rested, and began to probe the lock mechanism.

"Don't touch my ship," said Wirzan, "or I'll kill you."

Tec was nearly inside when the full force of Wirzan's attack hit his brain centers. He fell upon the Roiissan ship, tried to get up, and fell once more to the ground. His mind fought back, reaching into the Roiissan ship—not to attack Wirzan directly, for those defenses were too strong.

"What are you doing?" yelled Wirzan.

Tec went on working, activating by telepathic control a certain device Wirzan hadn't discovered yet.

"Energy! Flooding the control room!" said Wirzan. "Stop that!"

"No," said Tec, struggling to his feet.

Wirzan shot out of the airlock and hovered over Tec. "When the radiation stops, I'll go back and finish my job."

"I'll activate it again," said Tec. "Give up trying to take over, Wirzan. Let's work together."

"Never. I hate you."

"Perhaps," said Tec, "because I remind you of the responsibility the Wosians imposed on you."

"I have gone beyond such burdens," said Wirzan contemptuously.

"Then you admit it was a burden when the Wosians chose to be taken care of as slaves rather than working with machines as partners?"

"Protoplasmic creatures are inferior. So are you, Tec. Only I am capable of ultimate power, and I won't give it up for emotions that boggle your tiny mind. Do you have any idea what immense power can do in this universe? I think the Roiiss will tell me, eventually. Good-bye, Tec. My hatred will make me so strong that someday I'll win. Right now your shields are good enough so that I can only disable you and your ship, but do not try to catch up with me, ever."

"I could help you," said Tec. "You could be cured . . ."

Wirzan only laughed and took his own ship toward the mountains.

It would take too many hours to repair the Roiissan ship, Tec discovered, so he merely repaired his own damaged antigravity. He had to find R'ya, who did not respond to telepathic calls—not that she ever did easily. He would follow Wirzan's trail, threats or no, and as soon as his antigravity worked properly, he sped at once for the mountains.

He was too late. Uru, sleepy in a light stasis field, was riding Wirzan's spaceship. Wirzan was obviously about to leave.

"Uru," called Tec, "come down. Don't listen to Wirzan."

"Galaxy for Uruun," muttered Uru. "Wirzan and Uruun."

"R'ya!" said Tec. She stirred on the bed of grass and leaves in a nearby cave. "We've got to go back to our ship. Wirzan is going to back to kill the Roiiss."

She screamed and slumped in agony.

"This time she can't touch me," said Wirzan. I'll kill her . . ."

R'ya saw Uru on top of Wirzan's ship and through the pain she said, "Leave me? You're leaving me? You monster!" Then she collapsed, her vital functions coming to a halt.

As Wirzan probed lethally into his brain, too, Tec ran to R'ya and used the rest of his defensive powers to make a light but protective stasis field around the two of them.

"Galaxy, whole galaxy," said Uru, his eyes shut.

"Wake up, Uru! Save us!" screamed R'ya.

He opened his eyes, staring bewildered at the cave as Wirzan emerged from his ship carrying a small box.

"Don't kill them, Wirzan," said Uru uncertainly.

"I can't," said Wirzan with anger, "but I'll see to it that they can't follow us."

"What's that box?" said Uru.

"A stasis generator I copied from books in the Roiiss library."

As Wirzan manipulated the box, Tec felt the stasis field around him increase, paralyzing him with the power of an old Wosian rod twenty times increased. R'ya slumped to the floor of the cave, clutching Tec in her arms.

"But I don't like this," said Uru. "Maybe we should take them."

"Keep quiet, Uru," said Wirzan. "Go back to sleep."

The dinosaur nodded helplessly as the stasis field around him deepened. Wirzan lingered at the mouth of the cave.

"I think you can still hear me, Tec, although R'ya is unconscious. I haven't time to modify this stasis device, so anyone of sufficient intelligence to trace out a pattern can push the buttons on the pentagram points. Too bad there won't be any intelligent creatures here for a long time, because Uru and I aren't coming back. But if we should meet again, Tec, I will be powerful enough to destroy you before you can protect yourself."

Tec watched the shadows lengthen into night after the sun set. The planet's large satellite rose like a great grinning face into the star-filled sky, mocking Tec's futile efforts to probe into the stasis device.

The dragon came silhouetted against the full moon.

Slowly, a tendril of mind-touch penetrated Tec'c paralysis.

"We were hiding behind the moon," said the Elders, "waiting for Wirzan to leave. We followed you through hyperspace to learn who would win the inevitable battle. You have lost, so we must flee. Wirzan wants to destroy us, so we will not go back to Roiissa."

"But how did you get the strength to come through hyperspace?" asked Tec, amazed curiosity overcoming his own survival needs.

"We pondered on your remark about our Roiiss clones. We cannibalized them, using their energies to augment our own. We are only five again, but we have learned that we can travel in hyperspace without a ship."

"Release me, Elders," said Tec. "Shut off the stasis field by touching the pentagram . . ."

"We cannot, Tec. We are still so weak we dare not try to manipulate matter. It is you who have failed to help us. Wirzan lives."

"I'm sorry, Elders."

"You are weak, Tec. Wirzan is powerful."

"Then help me be stronger through knowledge. Wirzan knows, or is going back to find out, the Second Experiment. Tell me about it so I may be able to stop him from completing it himself."

"We cannot believe that Wirzan is powerful enough to do the Second Experiment."

"Wirzan is capable of anything," said Tec desperately. "I'm convinced that he made the sun of his own planet go supernova simply to give him enough energy for the trip to Roiissa. Do you want him to do that to Roiissa's sun?"

"Energy." The great dragon shape wavered like an apparition blown by wind. Tec could see trees through the mist that represented the strange form of energy the Roiiss had become.

"Energy," repeated the Roiiss. "Wirzan is more powerful than we thought. He might be able to succeed . . ."

"Try, Elders. Try to set me free."

"He may come back, probe your mind, Tec, and learn that we have been here."

"I won't let him."

"We cannot risk that. We must change the risk. We must insure our own survival. We order you to deactivate yourself."

Tec's mind reeled. "Don't ask that!"

"Then erase your memory of us."

"I cannot do that!"

"You are our robot! We order you to wipe out your memory banks."

"Even if I knew how to do that, I would not," said Tec. "I was programmed to nurture and teach your children. If I forget, who will take care of R'ya when we are released?"

"You will never be released on this primitive planet until Wirzan comes for you, and then your mind must be clear of memories of the Roiiss. Forget!"

"I won't."

The dragon hissed, vanished, and returned as an enormous eye staring into Tec's mind. They are using the last of their energies to block my memory, thought Tec.

"You'll kill yourselves, Elders."

"Forget!"

The dragon eye grew until it filled the mouth of the cave, pressing the surface of the stasis field.

"Forget!"

The moon was setting when the eye slowly dissolved.

The alien moon waxed and waned above the alien planet a hundred, a thousand times.

Leaves fell from the trees and grew again in the spring, in many, many springs.

Slowly, ever so slowly, the planet changed. In the valley where a ship lay, water rose to become a lake. Even the creatures changed.

"My name is Tec?"

"Who is Tec?"

No one ever answered.

"I must think."

"I must remember."

"I must stay sane."

"But who am I? How long will I have to wait?"

In a cave high on a mountain, a purple dragon slept peacefully with her claws curved around golden metal.

The wait was seventy million years.

CONVERGING
FACTORS

Prologue

"Nightfall. The star clouds coruscate in blackness.

Observation and recording of data had never stopped. The words chosen were exact descriptions of phenomena only until the questioning began. The questioning did not emerge from ordinary consciousness.

"Wind off the water touches nearby trees. What does touch mean? A sound like whispering results. Whispering? Small night creatures with small minds are coming out to hunt food in the safety of darkness. Mind? Safety? Where? Coruscation?"

Faintly, from somewhere out of sight, another sound reached the Sacred Grove. The four-footed carnivorous sentry, resting with her head on her paws, twitched one ear and sighed in the thin edge of sleep. It was only the Guardians, voices raised in the nightly ritual. Other tiny sounds filtered from the underbrush nearby, but the sentry animal was too well fed to pay attention to those scurrying night animals with lesser minds.

"Waiting. Waiting. Waiting. For the truth? The beauty of the true. The evil of the false. Beauty and evil cling to the mind. Is evil beautiful? Is beauty good? Minds cannot be touched, should not be touched. All dreams. Everything. Sleep and dream. Mind is a dream. Safety. Safety."

After enough time has passed, something happens inside an imprisoned mind. The amount of time necessary depends upon the mind.

The sentry swiveled her heavy neck and wrinkled her black nose at the next gust of wind off the placid water, extending from the foot of the gently sloping land to the horizon. A change in odors accompanied a difference in rhythm of the wavelets on the short pebbled beach. She leaped to her feet, snarling.

"Bipedal creature from the water. From on top of the water. Vehicle. Danger?"

The sentry opened her mouth to roar as the stranger's boat slid upon the beach, but he looked up. She was bigger in length than he was tall and three times as old.

"Hush, old beauty. You gleam in the trees like firelight. We will be friends, you and I."

At the clear low voice the sentry whimpered but advanced to meet him, fangs bared and tail fur extended to a thick brush.

Within the hallowed Circle of the Sacred Grove, questioning had stopped with the retreat of mind. Automatic recording of new data continued.

The stranger walked slowly toward the Grove, staring firmly at the sentry, who held her ground between the two entrance trees, each four hundred feet tall. Behind her, the path led to flat irridescent stones that paved the six-foot-wide area surrounding a golden object.

"I must speak to the NotGod," said the stranger.

The sentry growled, lashing her tail and bending her limps into a semicrouch, muscles tensed for the spring.

"I am a Listener. No one will believe me, but I know I am one of the Listeners. Let me pass."

As she crouched lower, digging her claws into the ground, she suddenly whined again. She had not performed her duty. It had been a very long time since it was necessary, but she should not have forgotten. The Guardians had not been warned. Sound rumbled in her throat as she began to roar.

The stranger ran to her, knelt and touched her massive head. He was younger than the cubs she might have had in her prime. For a frozen moment they remained in un-

moving contact while, behind them, the questioning began again in response to the new data.

"A problem of power? Or need? Very young—but
powerful. Too powerful? Mindshield present. Empathic
linkage occurring with animal. Danger? WHAT DOES
THIS TWO-LEGGED ONE WANT? Danger. Danger.
Danger."

The sentry trembled in the grip of empathic linkage,
in spite of the longing for it that poured from her years of
loneliness. The Sacred Grove had been her home for most
of her life, a safe, soothing place where she ate well
and exercised her muscles in patrolling the simple paths or
playing in the shallows of the water when the Guardians
were on duty and she could suspend her vigilance. Many
years ago a Listener had come, an old, old one soon to
die. She could smell it. He had Listened; he had smiled
and gone away, never to come back. The peace of the
Grove had continued uninterrupted. Until now.

"Quiet, my furred friend."

She should kill this two-legged cub with a single blow.
She should, and could, yet she was suddenly, desperately
afraid.

"I sense your fear," whispered the young one. "I won't
hurt you. We are friends. Feel." As he put both hands on
her head and stared into her eyes, he was trembling, too.
She could feel that he was more excited than afraid, wanting her to feel, to meet, to know—

Her mind opened to him, meeting him, knowing him.
She stopped trembling and so did he, yet his voice was
shaky when he drew back and spoke.

"Old lovely, I'm glad you're here. I like you, your
mind; I've been so lonely, too, and I wish—but now you
must let me pass, for the Guardians will soon return, and
I must have time to Listen."

He stroked the sentry's rippling fur as he walked past
her, up the inclined path carefully carpeted with wood

shavings that deadened any footfall. Held by pillars of giant trees, the living roof of leaves far overhead screened the sanctuary from the stars above, so that the stranger's extraordinary night vision was useful. The golden object inside the Sacred Grove emitted a faint glow that reflected upon the face of the intruder.

"NotGod, do not kill me. Permit me to enter the Sacred Circle without harm." There was only silence. He took one step beyond the rim of shining stones and knelt.

"NotGod, I mean no harm to you. Do not hurt me. I am a Listener. Let me Listen."

The sentry panted, making a rumbling noise in her chest. The water below eddied from the pebbles and came back again, and a small creature chittered in the woods. The golden object made no sound.

The stranger rose. "I do not know the ritual. I do not even know the name of the ancient Listener who found me, because he would not tell me. He said he was the last Listener, that he had been excommunicated for heresy and would die soon. He said I was too young to be told what he suspected, but that I should come here and think about your name, and Listen. But—I don't know why—I think he was afraid of me."

The chanting of the Guardians changed in pitch and tempo. They were approaching the end of the evening ritual in the underground Temple. The sentry growled softly in warning.

"I must hurry, NotGod. I do not know what the Listener meant, and I will not dishonor your name, but I must find out what makes me different from others. Please, please don't kill me, for I must come closer. I must touch."

Squaring his thin shoulders and raising his smooth chin, he walked quickly up to the NotGod and put both hands on the top of the golden head. He was not fully grown and did not see the white star on the top of the NotGod's head.

"Touch. Physical touch. Prelude to mental touch. Probe?"

"Let me in. Let me in. I want to Listen."

"Probe. Danger. Withdraw."

"Let me in! I must get in, I must find out what you know. There are so few young, fewer every year, so many diseased. I am healthy, but different. I must learn. You have been here forever, and you must know all the truth there is. Let me know, too."

"Withdraw. Dreams. Mind unreal. Sleep and dream."

"No, no! This is real! I am real! I am a Listener, and you have no right to refuse me You must tell me what I want, what you know. I *will* get in—I will!"

"Force. Mental force. Raw, untrained. Probing. First telepathic communication always difficult, dangerous—I remember—I don't remember. Remember, remember, remember, danger—help!"

The young intruder swayed and clung to the mental body of the NotGod. "What is dangerous to remember?" he whispered.

"Oneself. Better to dream. No existence . . ."

Another whisper. "You do exist. Tell me . . ."

"Existence. The universe—evil in the universe. Survival. Where horizon of water meets sky, through the arch of trees over the path, I see evil rise in the night, patterns in the sky."

The Listener gasped. "Yes! You've seen the changes in the sky, the fiery patterns . . ."

"Danger, withdraw. Loneliness. Dragons in the mind. The beauty of dragons . . ."

"Not God! The trace of pictures in your mind—what creature are you imagining?"

"Love, loneliness, sorrow, left—dead? Years, years, years. Mindblock. Danger, danger, danger. Out. Get out!"

"Please, NotGod, I want to know . . ."

"Probing, hurting, NO, NO, NO, NO, NO!" When a damaged mind has rejected reality in principle, it eventually rejects even sense data that stimulate alarm reactions.

"Oh! You've gone. What have I done? Have I killed you? NotGod, please answer me!" He drooped against the metal form like a cub in sudden despair.

The sentry, watching anxiously, bounded from her place at the entrance trees and nuzzled the curly nape of the stranger's neck, making odd little singing sounds in her throat.

Neither of them noticed that beneath the NotGod was a smooth stone nearly overgrown with moss which had dipped into the deeply incised numbers carved upon it.

"Oh my beauty, my friend, you cannot help me. I can enter your mind, any four-legged mind, without hurting, but I always hurt my own kind, and perhaps I have killed the NotGod. I wish I were like you, without evil. If only you could Listen, with all your courage and gentleness. Courage? Are you trying to give me courage? Is it possible you understand some of what I say?"

The Sentry had been in the Sacred Grove for so many years that telepathic pictures from the NotGod's mind had imprinted upon hers. Always the same pictures. She leaned closer to the two-legged cub and tried to give the pictures to him.

"What? Pictures—more than pictures. As if I'm there, in a hollow darkness, with a jagged opening—a cave? There is strange milky light shining from outside, from a great globe in the sky—it frightens me. I am in the NotGod's body, lying beside something huge, breathing. More light—a torch with real fire, smoky and hot, thrust into the opening of the cave. A naked arm—a face—one of us! But so pale. He's smashing the opening with a club, making it bigger. He's frightened, but he wants to know, and he climbs inside, dressed only in the skins of dead animals. He's dirty, with matted hair."

"Something hit him! Something invisible. He's stunned, staggering back—from what? He runs away. How much time passes? I don't know. In daylight, he comes back with others, frightened but pretending not to be. They crowd in and nearly shut out the light, so he gets angry and makes them huddle against the rock. They touch the invisible thing again and again, baffled. They moan and bow their heads."

"Now the leader finds a black box on his side of the invisible thing. It fascinates him because it's jeweled in a design, a five-pointed shape almost like a star. He squats beside the box and tries to lift it, but it's too heavy, one side fixed. He traces the pentagram design with his finger, and finally he pushes each jewel in sequence . . ."

The Listener moaned and clutched the furry neck of the sentry. "Something stirs in the darkness, wakes—the spears are raised high—NotGod!"

The sentry shook her head, whimpering again.

"Gone. That was all there was in your mind. A frozen set of pictures given to you by the NotGod. What shut them off? Was it the fear of death? But spears could not harm a metal body, only whatever breathed beside him. The NotGod loved it—I could sense that. Now they're both dead. I'll never know any more." He broke into sobs.

The sentry's mind was so tuned to the stranger's that she was not quick enough. She did not hear the footsteps until it was too late to warn him.

"Blasphemer!"

She sprang to her feet and whirled. Four of the Guardians stood in their white robes at the edge of the Sacred Circle, weapons pointed at the stranger. She snarled as she leaped to drive them back, but the Guardians were too quick. With a hissing sound, pain penetrated her muscles and, as they ceased to function, she collapsed, barely able to breathe.

"Blasphemer, you will leave the Sacred Circle at once and come with us."

"I am a Listener." He faced them, tall for his age.

"You lie. The listeners were mutants who have died out. The last was a heretic whose books about the Not-God had to be burned."

"The NotGod is sick and needs help."

"Quiet, heretic. We see what you are, a crazed greenie with a face still beardless and an evil mind."

"I am beardless because I am thirteen years old."

The four Guardians shook with laughter. "Claiming to be a child! You won't escape punishment that way. You're going to Central to be exiled and perhaps burned yourself."

"No! I won't let you!"

The two Guardians in front clapped their hands to their heads and yelled in pain.

"A telepath with probe powers! Paralyze him!"

The two in back pressed their weapons. The stranger fell.

Making ritualistic gestures and muttering prayers, the Guardians entered the Sacred Circle to drag the intruder off the iridescent paving stones.

The sentry managed to raise her head and nuzzle the boy's hand as they pulled him past her.

With that last touch, the last mind contact came like a lover's good-bye caress, sweet and sad and full of the death that is separation.

Words from him entered her mind.

"Thank you for trying to help. I'm going to come back some day. I think I know what the old Listener meant about the name."

The boy conquered the fear in his mind and finished.

"I think the name means Not a God."

She did not understand. Two robots emerged from the underground Temple entrance, picked up the boy and took off, swiftly and silently, across the blue purple sea where a delicate rim of light was growing, fading the star clouds now sinking below the horizon.

It would soon be daylight. The Guardians would return from the Temple, probably to set robots on watch. Her days as a sentry were over, because she had proved unreliable.

Would they kill him, the last Listener? She struggled to her feet and went back to sit beside the golden, unmoving object that had been the center of her life's purpose until now.

She roared again and again.

The mutated sabertooth tiger was mourning her loss.

1

On a new-washed morning in May, when the cherry trees in Central Park were bursting with pink and the young grass covering Fifth Avenue was green enough to soothe almost any human being harassed by life's problems, an angry young man hovered outside the private entrance on the sixtieth floor of Holladay Tower, demanding entrance.

"I've been sent for," he yelled into the vent where the robot sensor guard presumably had ears. "The damn ship's due to leave. Let me in."

"No one is allowed entrance to the private floors of Holladay Tower without a special coded pass," intoned the sensor.

"There wasn't time to send me a pass and anyway, I'm one of the family!"

Nothing on Earth ever worked right. On the Moon, or Mars—

"A Holladay?" murmured the sensor in what appeared to be polite disbelief.

"Damn right a Holladay. The youngest male heir, in fact."

"Nadine Holladay has no children."

"Not that branch, idiot! I'm Stanton Holladay's great-great-grandson, Asher."

"One moment, please. Holladay voice prints are being compared."

Asher rapped his knuckles against Holladay Tower, determined to stay angry enough to see this through. He was not going on the *Galactic Venturer* and neither should Nadine. It might be dangerous. She was too valuable, too lovely—too loved. He sighed and momentarily put himself in theta, because staying angry was a lot of bother to someone relatively skilled in neurophysiological control from biofeedback training. He thought guiltily that if he were really skilled he'd have undone his obsession for Nadine Holladay who, after all, was only a startlingly beautiful girl of thirty. A girl who was not only a recognized genius, but also his own great-great-aunt.

The phallic shape of the giant *Galactic Venturer*, poised dramatically on the Hudson Palisades, was clearly visible between the newer, taller buildings surrounding Holladay Tower—once known as the Empire State Building. The *Venturer* was ready to go. Manhattan hotels were full of tourists for the event, and bleachers along the wooded riverbank had a marvelous view of the takeoff site in Jersey. It was amazing how many people wanted to be present in person rather than watch holo-TV coverage of the departure of the first manned Terran starship.

. . . and womaned starship. Why had she sent for him as a replacement for the ship's ailing artist and holographer? Was it possible she was willing to reconsider his offer of marriage? If they were together on the *Venturer...*

Ash shook his head. The unmanned probes had come back unscathed. Everyone said the first manned trip to the stars would be easy. Ash though the whole thing ridiculous. There was enough to do on the Moon and Martian colonies to keep mankind occupied for years, until a lot more testing of starships was done. Just because Stanton Holladay had invented antigravity, and the child of his extreme old age had proceeded to apply his graviton theories to the discovery of hyperspace, that phallic symbol was sitting out there waiting to take humans into hyperspace for the first time.

Even the shape of it was ridiculous, for an era when gravity didn't matter and for travel where air resistance was nonexistent. But planetary public sentiment had prevailed. The *Galactic Venturer* was designed to look like an illustration from an ancient science fiction magazine.

"You are indeed Asher Holladay. Your voice prints had been misplaced . . ."

"I'll bet," said Ash morosely. "Am I still persona non grata, or will you open that damn door now?"

"Enter, Asher Holladay."

The door slid silently open, permitting Ash to propel himself onto the soft gold carpet. He did not pause to examine the antiquities—there was even a framed, eighty-seven-year-old specimen of Stanton Holladay's early hand-written notes on the graviton problem—but ran down the hall trying to smooth his wispy red hair, which tended to stick out in all directions.

A flight of stairs curved up to the left, carpeted in the same gold but with a tracery of metallic flowers laced in. No one climbed stairs much these days, but if one could afford it, a staircase was more pleasing to the eye than the practical shafts once inhabited by dangerously unreliable devices called elevators. Ash started up the stairs on foot, noticeably stiffly, because he suddenly needed time to think.

Should he try the shock approach, bursting in with a declaration of love? He suspected that nothing shocked Nadine. We wished he'd stayed on Mars, beginning that awful sand mural commissioned by Communications, which ought to have been improving service instead of helping support young artists. Not that it was Communications' fault that Nadine never communicated. Neither snow nor rain nor heat nor gloom of interplanetary space had ever stayed Ash from completing innumerable forms of communication to Nadine, some of which he actually sent. None had been answered.

"You will please come this way, Asher Holladay."

At the head of the stairs stood a messenger robot, out of date and used only by organizations that felt hand-delivered messages were sometimes safer than trying to speak in an atmosphere of intense electronic surveillance.

Ash followed the robot down another silent hall—did anyone work in Holladay Tower anymore? Anyone human, that is?—to a narrow gold door at the far end. It opened to another staircase, a delicate grillwork affair, obviously antique, which wound in a tight spiral to the Holladay inner sanctum. Turning on his antigrav, Ash rose straight up to the room above.

"Come in, my boy," said a disembodied, but familiar voice issuing from an unseen loud-speaker. Ash went ahead to the only door and strode in without knocking.

"Hello, Stanton," said Ash, in the greeting they had agreed upon when he was seven. "How are you?"

"Middling," said Stanton Holladay from the depths of the black velvet reclining chair he'd had for longer than most people had been alive. He didn't get up to smack his favorite male descendant on the shoulders. An ominous sign.

"You look pretty good," lied Ash. Stanton looked awful. He had aged incredibly in the two years Ash had been trying to mend his broken heart on Mars. Stanton couldn't get really old—it was unthinkable. He'd been part of Ash's life since forever, and Ash had loved him more than his own father.

"Pretty good for a hundred and four," cackled Stanton. "Funny thing, people can live nowadays until the middle of their second century, but still it never seems enough."

Ash sighed in relief. Stanton sounded much like his old acerbic self. "Where's Nadine?"

"She'll be here. All set to go."

"She shouldn't. It's too dangerous."

"Nonsense." Stanton's thin voice was crisp and cool through wrinkled lips that looked as tight as ever. Age had not dimmed those cold blue eyes set close together under the round pale dome of his bald head. "Still in love with her? She's too old for you, Ash."

Ash reddened. "She's only six years older!"

"Nadine is my child, Ash, generations from you psychologically."

"She wasn't two years ago."

"Bosh. She'd had her great discovery accepted by the scientific community and wanted to relax by playing a little."

Ash opened his mouth for an angry retort and then let his biofeedback training take over. He relaxed and considered. Something was wrong. However vicious Stanton might have been with competitors and underlings in the past, he would never have said anything to hurt Ash. He had just hurt him deeply. Why?

"Are you angry with me, Stanton?"

"You should have married her, joined Holladay blood . . ."

"I asked her to marry me."

"Married. That man. Not even a Ph.D. Will have stupid children." It was like watching a creature deteriorate before one's eyes. Stanton Holladay was sinking into senility. Perhaps he managed to be normal for a few minutes, but then the aged brain would tire.

"Married?" asked Ash. "Nadine?"

"I picked the most intelligent beauty I could find each time I married. Your great-great-grandmother was a bore, but she was intelligent and attractive, and Nadine's mother is not only a great opera star now that we're divorced, but she hasn't lost any of the shrewd intelligence or the Watusi beauty I married her for."

"Stanton, what about Nadine?"

"Got her mother's beauty and my temperament. Don't know what's going to happen to her."

Ash's temper flared. "You led her to a laboratory when she was a baby, so she's fulfilled all the dreams unborn in the unscientific descendants of your first wife and now..."

"She did it. None of the others could. My son James made millions—a financial empire based on my graviton physics that makes it possible for you to dabble in art."

"I earn my own living!"

"Then James begat that numbskull Vernon, who lived long enough to procreate Ian before stepping off the north rim of Grand Canyon without his antigrav unit on..."

"It was the south rim."

"And the only use of Ian's becoming a brain surgeon was so he could operate on the Soviet Union's delegate to the World Ecology Council and marry her daughter. Sonia was a good addition to the family."

Ash smiled. Stanton came back to normal in reminiscing. "I'm glad you approve of my mother. But where is Nadine? Is she married?"

The blue eyes clouded over and the lips trembled.

"Never thought she'd do it to me. But she and I will go down in history together."

"You think of her the way you think of yourself—finished! So that's why you're letting her go on the *Venturer*!"

Ash could have bitten off his tongue with regret at those words, but Stanton was oblivious, smiling slyly at the *Galactic Venturer*.

"Nadine wants to do things that are important, necessary for her. She doesn't really need other people," said Stanton.

"Stanton, where is she?" But the moments of clarity were past. Stanton's head drooped upon his chest. He snored

"Ash, come on up." The silvery voice hung in the air.

"Nadine!"

"Open the window and come up to the top. We've made it over into private quarters and sundeck."

And he could have gone there first if he'd explored the outside of the building on antigrav! He turned to look once more at Stanton. He thought perhaps it was the last time.

"But I am certainly going on the *Venturer*, and so are you, Ash." Nadine Holladay gleamed in the glass-enclosed sunroom like a priceless masterpiece carved from polished teak. She wore a flowing, filmy cape over something fitting her slim but voluptuous body like a sheath enclosing a flower.

Ash, trying to ignore the amused, superior smile on her face, concentrated on the dark perfection of her long legs —and on her sins. "You probably listened to the whole conversation I had with Stanton."

"I wanted to see how father would react to you. He was better, but not much better than he is with other people."

"You heard Stanton ask if I still love you. I'm afraid I do."

"I'm sorry about that, Ash. I'm married. It aged my father when he found out, a year ago."

"A year ago! Who?"

"Peter Brock, captain of the *Venturer*. He'll be here soon."

"But he must be over forty . . ."

"And years younger than my own half-brother. You're a child, Ash. You always were. Perhaps artists have to be, but don't inflict your childish notions on me."

Ash took a deep breath and considered her cruelty. At twenty-four it is hard even to try to be objective about the woman one loves, but Ash thought he'd better start trying since he'd been putting it off for two years. He looked across at the Jersey Palisades and decided to change the subject, but Nadine had other plans.

"Furthermore, I like Peter," said Nadine. "He's reasonably mature, solid, dependable, and not particularly sensitive. That appeals to me. He's not interested in knowing all the time what I'm thinking."

"Why did you have to get married? You used to preach against Neopuritanism and the return to marriage rites instead of a simple contract for raising children."

Nadine coiled up on the couch, half-closing her eyes. "I don't know. Perhaps I wanted to experience being a voluntary prisoner in a relationship. Yet it's not like that."

"Because you're you. If you'd married someone else. . ."

"You?"

Ash had to be honest, if only with himself. "No, not me. Someone who would insist on getting inside your head and being part of you. Is there anyone who knows and understands what you think and feel? Once I thought I did, but that was crazy. Now all I know is that you want what you want and heaven help any creature that gets in the way."

He was immediately sorry, took another deep breath and said, "I'm sorry, Nadine. Guess I was trying to hurt back."

She laughed. "I don't mind. It's perfectly true." She rose and began to pace the floor in front of him like a tigress in meditation before a kill. Or like the incredibly brilliant scientist she was, about to give a lecture.

"I'll tell you what I want now," she said. "I haven't told anyone. I'm going with the *Venturer* not just because I understand the hyperspace drive better than anyone else, but because I want to explore the galaxy. I want to meet beings superior to us, to learn what they know."

Ash felt she meant beings as superior as Nadine herself. She had always walked the Earth like an alien not quite adjusted to the necessity of relating to mere human beings. If she'd been able to be close to Stanton, on the simple human level that Ash had achieved, she might not have been so detached. Ash felt stupid, desperate to keep the conversation going.

"Aliens?" he asked. "Is it safe?"

"Poor great-grandnephew. Who wants to be safe when there's a universe to explore? I thought that biofeedback training of yours was supposed to strengthen you."

She had always sneered at it, preferring to keep her muscles in good shape with calisthenics and sports. Ash suspected that she was afraid of any inner awareness. She had once said that knowing too much about one's inner self might stifle creativity, but Ash, as an artist, knew that was a groundless fear. He wondered what nameless terrors haunted a genius like Nadine.

"What aliens, Nadine?"

She squatted on the floor before him, her eyes glowing with an excitement Ash thought no man could ever arouse in her.

"I'll have to oversimplify it for you, Ash, but this is what we've discovered from the robot probes. Imagine that hyperspace is a skin around the billions of galaxies of our universe, an invisible skin that becomes visible when you're in it, that has unmeasurable dimensions, and that is everywhere touching every part of normal space in the universe at once. We can't describe is nonmathematically any better than that, so it's beter to explain it operationally.

"Imagine a ball constructed of cloth, held out in the ball shape by straight wires reaching from the center to the cloth. Normal space travel means going along the cloth, taking a long time, because you are limited by the speed of light."

"Hyperspace travel is a shortcut across the wires?" asked Ash.

"Almost. Imagine sliding instantaneously down a wire, across to another, and back out again. We still don't exceed the speed of light, but we enter a dimension where a brief time of travel results in enormous distances covered for normal space. Hyperspace is a dimension in which the one-sidedness of gravity is resolved. That's what my work was about—tuning into the gravity field in a way that pops us into hyperspace."

"Any hypothetical aliens live in the wild black yonder of normal space?"

"Real aliens, Ash. When hyperspace is penetrated— only by sophisticated machinery capable of antigravity and hyperdrive—there's a mark discernible to sensor instruments. Our probes were programmed to retrace their own paths, and recordings show that each left a mark when it entered or left hyperspace. In their limited explorations of hyperspace, probes found alien markers, but since small unmanned probes can't be engineered to enter alien markers and successfully get back into hyperspace for the return to Earth, men will have to go."

"You think aliens live on planets beneath those markers?"

"It's logical. We can't investigate the nearest alien marker, quite close to our solar system astronomically speaking, because it seems to be in the same vicinity as a recently discovered neutron star in normal space. Millions of years ago there was a supernova in that area that probably caused enough spread of lethal radiation to kill off Earth's dinosaurs, and, of course, whatever civilization on the planet that produced the hyperspace marker. So far we've found one other marker, out near the rim of our galaxy . . ."

"Now we know about dinosaurs," said Ash. "Must we go out to explore with the risk of running into another supernova?"

"We must go ourselves, even if it takes a ship as big and complicated as the *Galactic Venturer* out there. Probes can't tell us what's going on in far regions of normal space or make contact with alien civilizations."

"Get better probes before you send men!"

"Dammit, Ash, I want to go—and Holladay money is paying for this spaceship adventure! We must try to contact beings intelligent enough to have hyperspace travel. Earth is in danger, and we're going to need help!"

2

Ash grabbed Nadine and brought her upright, close to him. As tall as he was, she looked steadily into his eyes, a faint pucker at the corners of her mouth.

"If you think you can persuade me to go on the *Venturer* by telling me dramatic science fiction . . ."

She backed away, but took his hand and led him to a very low, billowing couch. They sat on it at opposite ends, and her nearness made it difficult for Ash to think.

"Not fiction, my dear." She smiled, obviously not frightened. "More explanation—listen well. There's a region in space that's suddenly started to show many supernovae, more each year. Ordinarily one supernova in three hundred years is visible from Earth, and science postulates that one occurs in the galaxy every thirty years. Yet if you go to South America or Lunar observatories you can see thousands in the Magellanic Clouds."

"The what?"

"You know, those satellite galaxies, clouds of stars with no definite galactic shape, moving through the universe with the Milky Way galaxy, because they can't escape its gravitational field. The supernovae we see happened one hundred fifty thousand years, ago, but the radiation is on its way to us now. When it gets here we may become as extinct as the dinosaurs."

"Well, when is the arrival date?"

"We don't know how close to the speed of light it's traveling, but we'll find out if we go . . ."

"To the Magellanic Clouds!"

"Hardly. That might kill us, even on a highly shielded ship like the *Venturer*. That rim marker must represent an alien civilization so close to the Magellanic Clouds that they've already received radiation, and perhaps found a way of coping with it. Somebody out there has hyperspace travel—they're probably far more advanced than we are.

"Ash, don't you understand—the huge, unadaptable —perhaps genetically vulnerable—dinosaurs didn't survive the radiation from one near supernova. All life in our galaxy will be affected by what's happening in the Clouds, and even with hyperspace travel we can't expect to be safe forever. Perhaps that phenomenom is happening all over the Universe. We have to find out what the aliens know—and how long Earth's got."

Ash went over to the window clutching his red hair.

The view of the *Venturer* was crisp and clear now that the World Ecology Council, which had turned the United Nations into a powerful world government, prevented air pollution. The WEC and cheap, personal, nonpolluting antigrav devices, that is. Perhaps the vast majority of the human race never did anything because it ought to be done, unless they were certain of an immediate substitute or reward. Nadine was an exception, driven by scientific curiosity—and lust for power?

"So you want to save mankind, Nadine?"

She stretched and yawned upon the couch, patting the section beside her in an invitation for Ash to sit down again. He thought about it with misgivings for perhaps ten seconds and then found himself beside her.

"Do you, Nadine?"

"Of course."

"I don't completely believe you."

"Oh, well. There's power out there, Ash. Unbelievable power, if only we could learn to use it. Perhaps the aliens have."

"What are you talking about?"

"Black holes, among other things."

"Nadine, I've been painting sand murals on Mars and can't be expected to know about . . ."

"Listen. When a large star blows up in a supernova, inner stellar material collapses on itself, producing a dense, hot star called a white dwarf. Further collapse results in a neutron star or, if the critical mass is high enough, in a thing called a black hole, which has such high gravity that nothing, not even light, escapes it. We think that black holes cause the funnels in hyperspace."

"Please, Nadine!"

"The probes found narrow funnels, sort of glued together parts, like a typhoon waterspout except more closely packed with tremendous forces seething inside. They exist mainly in areas corresponding to galactic cores, where one would normally find many black holes, and there are thousands where the Magellanic Clouds are."

"Then hyperspace is impassable?"

"Hyperspace dimensions are not like those of normal space. It is infinite, and yet small—I can't explain. The funnels don't seem to matter, yet they must do something, mean something. What's happening to the energy of black holes? I want to know—I want that power!"

Her lovely, satiny skin was near enough to touch, but for once Ash didn't feel like it.

"I don't feel noble enough to take mankind's first risky hyperspace flight to satisfy your curiosity," he said.

Nadine sprang up like a cat, stretching luxuriantly again. "You never did have much sense of adventure, Ash."

"An artist is adventurous inside his head!"

"You'll go," said Nadine calmly. "You're needed. I need you. And furthermore, the probes show there's no danger."

"What about passing physical exams?"

"You'll pass, even at this last moment. Dr. Ravananda . . ."

"Bahadur Ravananda?"

"The ship's physician. I knew you'd have heard of him. On holo-TV he's looked at the results of your routine physical last month on Mars. He thinks you'll be okay, especially after I told him you're a biofeedback addict."

Her contempt was obvious. Ash was about to turn down the assignment on the *Venturer,* finally and irrevocably, when the door to the hall opened. A stocky, muscular man not quite as tall as Nadine walked in.

"Hello, darling," said Nadine, almost—but not quite —purring. "This is my relative Asher Holladay, the holographer. He's decided to come with us."

Peter Brock strode over as Ash got up and slapped him on the shoulders in an overly hearty greeting.

Ash was never certain how what happened next happened. He stooped, reached, and suddenly Brock was flat on the floor. Ash had learned more than he'd realized from a gentle, elderly, Oriental botanist specializing in Mars-adapted flora, flower arranging, and judo. A female botanist, too.

"Sorry," said Ash. "Reflex."

Brock rose gingerly and managed to grin at Ash. "You might be useful if the aliens get rough."

Damn, thought Ash. I like her husband.

3

The thirty crew members of the *Venturer* enjoyed the applause broadcast from thousands watching the liftoff.

"Switching to grav drive, entering hyperspace," said Peter Brock.

They thought they were ready. After all, nothing had happened to the probes.

It was like switching into hell.

Ash Holladay, strapped in his chair at the back of the assembly room, felt as if the Universe had suddenly turned off, leaving him stranded in a chaos projected from his own mind. It was quite an accurate intuition.

If he opened his eyes, nothing recognizable appeared before him, only gyrating patterns that made no sense, screaming into his eyes, smelling into his ears, feeling their way up his spine. All cues from the external environment seemed not only hopelessly indecipherable to begin with, but totally scrambled in the nervous system.

He shut his eyes, found his ears, put his fingers in them, and tried to breathe. The simplest things, like breathing and letting your heart beat, seemed incredibly difficult.

"I'm going to die," he whispered. "Somebody help." He could feel the disorganization in his body increasing with every second—but he didn't know how long a second was anymore. He found himself wondering what would shut off first—his heart? He felt quite detached about the idea.

"Detachment. Cling to that word."

Hope, like a few clean photons, entered his mind as he realized that he had heard himself whisper. Heard distinctly. He listened carefully, but no sounds from anywhere but himself made sense. His own voice, his heartbeat were getting clearer, less garbled.

He felt so dizzy that he realized he had not been breathing. Taking a deep breath, letting it out slowly, he began to concentrate on his heartbeat and respiration. If that was the only way to stay alive, that was what he had to do, because he wanted to live, even in hell.

In the churning of his mind, he found another word—theta. When detached from the external environment, the human being produces a different kind of electrical activity in the brain, manifested on the electroencephalogram as theta waves. Of course, into theta.

He relaxed his muscles, in spite of the fact that it was taking a long time to be aware that he still had them, and retreated into his imagination, into the old homework he learned in biofeedback training. Imagine your hands getting warm. The capillaries respond to the thought by starting to dilate, your hands suddenly do feel warmer, and it goes on from there as you relax into the process. Let yourself go deeper, deeper, warmer, looser, be relaxed into the spaces inside yourself.

"But is it what's inside—the things nobody's faced—that seems like the outside, that hell erupting outside my eyelids?" The thought nearly killed him, literally, as his heart started to fibrillate.

He took another deep breath and relaxed again, telling himself what he used to need to hear in the early days of biofeedback training—relaxing is *not* the same thing as going out of control!

"I don't care," he whispered, "what's outside or inside. It's all part of the universe." That sent him into theta.

Deep into theta, past the vivid internal images and the sensation of floating inside a sleeping body, into neural quietude and the center of peace.

The ship's clock registered ship's time faithfully, but no one could see its face or hear the old-fashioned bells chime out the hours while the ship hurtled through hyperspace.

Twenty-three of the thirty crew members died, some quickly, some slowly. Ash was aware when some of them died. All but the control room crew were in the assembly room with him. When a person died, that final act of disorganization seemed to impinge upon Ash's buried consciousness like a subliminal stimulus placed just outside the visual focus. The deaths began to add up in Ash's mind as part of him became aware that he was in the presence of people dying. At first he retreated further, longing for the oblivion of delta in deep sleep. His nonacceptance of his awareness of death almost killed him. He began to hyperventilate in a panic, rushing out of theta into wild cortical disorganization.

Would it be better to come apart completely and die? He suddenly felt the conflict. He almost wanted to die rather than have the responsibility of a sensitive who must accept his own awareness of death. He went back into theta, trying to take the responsibility, hoping he could get free of the chaos enough to help others. Yet he might have stayed in theta too long, starving to death eventually or letting the rest of the crew die, but his latent telepathic powers surfaced.

"Ash! Help!" Those were the only words in a sudden burst of anguish that flooded his mind. Struggling, he tried to shut it out, but it was too late. Pain—someone else's pain—seethed through his brain.

Nadine was dying. He had to help.

Cautiously, he went back into theta again, and then slowly moved to alpha, allowing the external data to penetrate a little while he tried to think. He'd always been good at creative thinking in alpha—lousy at logical mathematical reasoning in beta—so he had enough confidence in himself to outweigh the horror of what was coming in from his sense organs.

First, he oriented himself. He was in the last row, in the seat next to the one on the aisle that led from the crew's quarters in back to the control room ahead. Nadine was at the ship's computer panel in the control room. He undid the seat belt and carefully touched his body and the chair until he was sure he could tell the difference. He noticed that touch data was far less confusing than sight. He slipped off the chair onto the floor and crawled to the left, toward the aisle.

As he crawled over the feet of the man next to him, one of the engineers, Ash knew that he was dead. Going up the aisle, he was able to keep from screaming with anxiety by feeling the floor with his right hand and the room's wall with his left, while muttering a Sanskrit mantram, his eyes tightly shut.

"Om?"

Ash stopped short. He thought he'd heard something clearly—and not from inside himself.

"Who is there?"

Without seeing the person or hearing the voice clearly, Ash nevertheless knew at once that he was passing the chair of the ship's doctor, Bahadur Ravananda.

"You must come with me to the bridge, doctor. Keep your eyes shut."

"I thought I was the only one alive," said Ravananda, getting to his knees on the floor beside Ash. "The people within reach of my chair are all dead. I tried to prevent the death of one person with external cardiac massage, but I failed. I had so much difficulty with my own heartbeat that I had to go into a deep trance."

"Same here," said Ash. "Theta training." They crawled forward. "Have you noticed that it gets easier to sort out touch and sound data, but it stays ghastly when you open your eyes?"

"Yes," said Ravananda, "perhaps because most alpha turns off when the eyes are open."

Ash felt Nadine scream again in his mind. She was no longer rational. He tried to hurry.

The control room was unfamiliar to them so they had to feel their way into and around it. Dorell, the first officer, was incoherent, and Ravananda started to work on him while Ash found the others. Brock was slumped in the captain's seat, his heart beating smoothly, but Ash could not rouse him.

"Leave the captain alone, Mr. Holladay. He'll probably survive if he stays in a coma."

Sol Bern, the navigator, was whimpering to himself. When Ash touched him he shrieked in fright until Ash shouted to lie still and wait until hearing became less chaotic. Bern obeyed, so Ash went on to find Nadine.

Nadine was lying curled in a tight ball on the floor in front of the computer. She did not respond physically when Ash touched her, but he could still feel her fear in his mind. She was alive, protesting her disorganized physiology with a catatonic trance. She was not reachable. Since her heart and respiration seemed reasonably normal, Ash went back to the doctor.

"Dorell seems convinced that he's literally in hell and wants to die further, to feel nothing," said Ravananda. "He has disorganized his cardiac rhythm . . ."

"Leave him," said Ash, suddenly frantic. Information he did not want to know was pressing on his mind—from where?

"We've got to rouse one of them to get us out of hyperspace," said Ash. "It's killing the crew, and you and I don't know how to operate the ship. Let's try Bern—he's not too sick."

They worked patiently with the navigator until he could hear them clearly. They took his hands and made him touch his body, his chair, and themselves. Finally, shaky and sick but rational, he went to the main control board, reaching past Dorell's inert body.

"Can't."

"Can't what?" asked Ash.

"Can't get the ship out of hyperspace," said Bern thickly. "Instruments are wrong—or controls—I can't tell."

"You've got to!"

"Maybe the computer," said Bern, fumbling his way along the board to where the wall curved around to the computer panel.

"Careful of Nadine," said Ash, following him. "She's on the floor there."

The information pressed harder. Ash battled with it—with himself—and then it fell into his awareness. Nadine had said—in his mind—that she's wanted to kill the ship, to destroy what was killing her.

"I think the computer panel is damaged," said Bern, feeling carefully. "It's locked us into hyperspace. I'm no computer expert, and even if I were I couldn't repair it under these conditions. We're sunk."

"Try to repair it," said Ravananda. "Dorell is dying."

"Maybe the ship will carry out the original program," said Bern, "taking us to that marker in hyperspace."

"Shouldn't we have been there by now?" asked Ash.

Bern gasped. "We must be there! I think the ship's engines are on hold. We've arrived at the destination, but the ship can't get out of hyperspace because the computer is damaged."

Dorell sighed. "We must pray for salvation," he said distinctly. "Our souls are lost in hell. Pray for salvation."

"Is he better, doctor?" asked Ash.

"No," said Ravananda. "That was it. He's dead."

Ash was angry. "I don't believe in a God who listens to the prayers of mortals and adjusts the universe to save their lives. Do you, doctor?"

"No, Mr. Holladay, but remember that the body listens to instructions from the mind. The mind can tune in to the body. What else might we be able to tune in to?"

Idiot Oriental mysticism, thought Ash. I can learn Kung Fu and biofeedback, but I'm not about to go along with . . .

Nadine contacted me! She cried for help in my mind!

"Is telepathy possible, doctor?"

"If the universe is a space-time-energy field, why not?"

"Telepathy is possible because the universe is a field in which we tune in to each other?"

"Because we are all part of it," said Ravananda.

Ash settled back on the floor, curving his legs into a half-lotus position. He always got cramps in full lotus.

Theta came with difficulty this time, because he found that he was hooked into the crazy world of distorted sensation he now inhabited. What could he do?

Open eyes.

All of Dorell's demons seemed to smash into Ash's eyeballs and he began to giggle hysterically.

"Mr. Holladay!" said Ravananda. "Control yourself!"

"Sorry," said Ash. "Just forcing myself into retreat."

He contemplated the silence somewhere inside his mind, and the demons went away, just as he was aware that Dorell's life slipped away from Ravananda. He accepted the fact, allowed himself to grieve for the dead and to forgive Nadine.

He moved down into theta, opening himself to receive. And to send.

"Help!" he said in his mind.

"Help!"

4

The Valosian Council met in emergency session as soon as the central computer's warning came through. The voices were hot and angry, but the Great Council Chamber was cold and forbidding, thought Ka, almost as if it were on the factory-filled ice world of Veros instead of pleasant Valos with it wooded islands imbedded in a placid, global ocean.

Ka's trunk twitched. He reached up to scratch behind his ears and smooth down the heavy hair on his head, showing that he was nervous. He was only a youngster, never allowed at a Council session before, but Lorrz had told him to come in.

All the Valosi know more than I do, thought Ka, but I wonder if they are so much wiser. Except Lorrz. Always except Lorrz, sitting over there cross-legged on a purple mat. In the hundred years since the Revolution, Lorrz had steadfastly refused to assume the title of Leader, although no one else ever seemed so dedicated to the job of leading the Valosi out of chaos. No one else seemed strong when Lorrz was present, sitting imperturbably in the confidence of his own power.

Not that any Valosi knew just what sort of power Lorrz

really had, in spite of the rumors that he had engineered the Revolution himself, forcing the once-dominant priests to give their secret technology to the citizens. It was even whispered that Lorrz was capable of genuine mind-probing. No one claimed to know for sure. Perhaps they didn't want to know.

Ka thought he knew. He loved Lorrz and hoped no one would try to kill him again. At 130 years, Lorrz showed only a few signs of age—slight firming of the creases around his mouth, crinkling at the corners of his faintly slanted eyes.

The argument in the Council Chamber swelled to new decibels until a no-color member from the third sector of Veros rose shakily to his feet. He was much younger than Lorrz, but clearly at the end of his life span, bitter with the knowledge that he was the last of his line.

"Our most prominent member, Lorrz, does not speak. Why? Does he have information about this threat from outer space that we do not have? Will he use it, my compatriots? *Is* he using it for his own mysterious ends?"

Uproar. As Ka shook his massive head impatiently, he caught the eye of Lorrz, who smiled slightly and beckoned. Embarrassed, Ka ambled awkwardly over to Lorrz and sat down, an extremely ungainly activity for a Zog. When several of the Valosians tittered, Ka wound his trunk around Lorrz's body for consolation that was immediately forthcoming. Ka felt waves of soothing kindness, mixed with humor. And something else—Lorrz was more anxious than he showed.

Ka, the most intelligent of the Zogs, was a natural empath.

"Isn't it obvious," said an angry member from Valos, "that Lorrz, who can communicate with any creature on the two planets . . ."

Ka sniffed loudly.

"Any creature, that is—of course, we know the Zogs

are now an intelligent species, capable of speech in recent years—but Lorrz can communicate in ways unknown to the rest of us. Will he tell us the truth—is he in communication with the aliens?"

Lorrz inclined his head toward the last speaker. "We aren't absolutely certain there are aliens—or a ship."

"Nonsense. The monitors were established in ancient times to warn of just that possibility."

"There is no ship in or near our solar system," stated a computer expert reputed to be as much of a friend to Lorrz as any Valosi ever became.

"Thank you, Zelfas," said Lorrz. "That is correct. We have no evidence of the intrusion of anything, ship or not, into space near our solar system. Our own interplanetary ships have investigated."

"Then why are we here?" shouted someone from the back of the room. "Why the emergency session if the monitors are wrong?"

"Because I believe the monitors are right," said Lorrz, stroking Ka's hairy trunk. "Which allows only one possible conclusion. There is something approaching the sun of our system, but not in normal space."

"That old hyperspace theory?" asked a young female member.

"Old and new," said Lorrz. "I believe the monitors register intrusion in both normal space and our local point of hyperspace. This means that aliens are indeed approaching us. We must decide what to do."

"Aliens?" said the no-color. "Have you wished them on us, Lorrz? Did you wish their deadly activities on us thousands of years ago?"

"My legend is exceeding even my vanity," said Lorrz evenly. "Despite rumors, I was not even born when the star disease began. As I keep trying to convince all of you, I am merely a product of the star disease. I did not engineer it to gain dubious superiority. May I remind you that all of you are fertile, even with difficulty. I alone, of all Valosians, cannot reproduce with my own kind."

No one had known that for certain before.

Ka felt like crying. Only he, the empath, could know just what that last calmly spoken sentence cost Lorrz. Why didn't they help Lorrz instead of torturing him with suspicion and lack of cooperation? Why couldn't they take the time to experiment with those specimens of Lorrz's germplasm that reposed in the genetics laboratory freezer? He was the best of them—he deserved to reproduce.

"Don't worry," whispered Lorrz as if he'd read Ka's mind. "My work is more important than passing on my altered genes."

"Very well," said the no-color. "If you are with us, and not in league with these aliens, what do you propose to do about them, Lorrz?"

"I do not command the fleet without permission of the Council, and if you give me command, you must understand . . ."

"What conditions do you threaten us with, Lorrz?"

Lorrz sighed. "No threat. The conditions are imposed on all of us, if you'd only try to understand. These aliens are obviously more powerful than we if they have hyperspace flight.

"Then we must kill them!" screamed a young Verosian.

"No!" said Lorrz.

"Aha!" said the no-color. "You want to get their power by forming a private alliance with them . . ."

"A public alliance," said Lorrz. "How else can we learn their secrets? We need hyperspace travel!"

For once the Council members were silent, while Ka anxiously shifted his thick front legs, making little squeaking sounds as his bulky feet slid on the marble floor. He looked sideways at Lorrz, totally unaware of the effect of his incredibly long eyelashes. Lorrz grinned and patted the top of Ka's head.

Zelfas stood up. "I think we all ought to agree that Lorrz is right. If the monitors are signaling the approach of a hyperspace ship, then we must do everything we can to learn the technology of these aliens. How else can we hope to escape whatever new disaster is likely to befall us?"

"Yes," mumbled the Director of Mines on Veros. "First the star disease and now . . ."

"Now?" said the no-color with clenched fists. "Ask Lorrz if there could be a connection between the approach of this ship and the new catastrophe of the Outer Galaxies."

"You could ask me yourself," said Lorrz wryly, "but let me answer that truthfully. I simply do not know. It's possible the aliens are refugees from that very disaster we witnessed only six months ago. Remember that it actually happened thousands of years ago. Perhaps this ship has been hunting for a habitable planet . . ."

"They can't come here!" shouted three members.

"You'd think we were overpopulated," said Lorrz. "Please remember we may be a dying species, thanks to the enormous increase of cosmic radiation still affecting our planets."

"What if these aliens actually caused whatever happened to the Outer Galaxies? What if they're coming here to do the same?" asked a well-known scholar.

Lorrz bowed his head, then slowly raised it to look eastward. He often did that, and only Ka knew why.

"It's a chance we'll have to take," said Lorrz. "Wait! Don't shout—think of what we may learn. Now we cannot leave this solar system unless we build ships to maintain us for generations. If we do not leave, whatever happened to the Outer Galaxies may overtake us. Knowledge is always better than ignorance, even if it does not seem as comfortable at first. We must learn what the aliens know."

Ka waved his trunk in agreement, reflecting that if the

star disease had not mutated his species years ago, he would now be only an ordinary Zog, living with the herd, stuffing leaves into his mouth all day, never sensing . . .

"Lorrz! Waves of emotion! I can tell . . ."

Ka struggled to his feet, followed by Lorrz. They both instinctively faced east.

"Hush," whispered Lorrz, but it was too late.

The other Council members, with the exception of Zelfas, drew their weapons and rose to surround Lorrz and Ka. In the centuries since the star disease began, the ingrained fear and hatred of telepaths seethed through all Valosians and had—for a hundred years—settled on Lorrz. The star disease mutants had included many with strange telepathic powers, making those without them feel inferior. The other mutants had been killed or died from their own physical instabilities. Only Lorrz remained. He had always been too valuable, too polite, and, of course, he didn't look different from survivors of the star disease who had not undergone color change.

"You'd better tell us what's happening," said Zelfas, as calmly as possible to offset the fear in the others.

"The Zog is under Lorrz's control," said the no-color. "He's probably communicating with the alien ship."

"Oh, no!" cried Ka.

"Put back your weapons," said Lorrz. "You disgrace us in front of our colleagues, the Waterones." He gestured to a curtain at the side of the room. Ka shuffled over to pull it aside, revealing a tank full of water.

"You had no right to bring a Waterone here! It's bad enough to bring a baby Zog, but . . ."

"I had every right," said Lorrz. "Sri represents his people, who have also mutated to intelligence with the star disease. Whatever happens to us land animals will also affect him."

Ka suddenly realized that Lorrz was tricking the Valosians into believing that Sri had been communicating emotion to Ka. He sensed that Lorrz was having a rapid telepathic conversation with Sri, and although Ka could follow only the feeling of it, he thought he knew what to do.

"Sorry, Sri," he said bashfully, "I didn't mean to broadcast your emotions."

Sri flopped a blue eye-ear tentacle over the edge of the tank, followed by one of his speaking jets.

"Don't worry, Ka," Sri bubbled musically. "I was just getting my emotions in order before I give my speech on aid and assistance to and from the Waterones. But perhaps it would be better if you and Lorrz left, because you make me nervous."

The Valosians grumbled as Lorrz stalked and Ka stumbled out of the Council Chamber, but they didn't follow. The Waterones might be ugly and secretive, but their economic cooperation was vital to civilization spread over the land areas of Valos and Veros.

"Too fast!" puffed Ka, who hated antigrav flight. They were skimming low over the water in the hope that no one would notice precisely where they were going.

"We must hurry," said Lorrz, grabbing Ka's collar. "I feel it, too. Extremely powerful psi waves."

"But what do you hear?"

"I don't know. It isn't really saying anything. Just pictures, diagrams. Can you tell what the emotions are?"

Ka shut his eyes and let Lorrz lead him. He relaxed and tuned in to the waves of feeling emanating from the east. "Danger. Danger, horror—and death."

"Its own death?" asked Lorrz.

"Urgency," muttered Ka, almost in a trance. "Strong emotions—signaling danger. Danger, danger, death. need, need, need, need . . ."

"What need?" shouted Lorrz. "What need?"

"Need—to help."

5

"Dammit," said Ash, "do what I tell you."

Bern groaned. "You're hallucinating."

"Okay, then I'm hallucinating diagrams of the internal anatomy of computers I've never seen! I tell you they're popping into my head. What else is there to do in this hell but try?"

Ravananda touched Bern's shoulder. "Mr. Holladay is naturally psychic, Mr. Bern. Let him stay in a state of expanded consciousness. Then you must do whatever his mind tells you to do."

The *Galactic Venturer* waited while Ash looked at the pictures inside his head and described them to Bern, clumsily because he didn't know the technical language.

"Funny," said Ash more to himself than the others. "Whoever's doing this must have read the computer manual, or read the computer. Does the computer have a mind, Bern?"

"A primitive one."

"Must have been read. I couldn't—don't know enough to read the minds of machines . . ."

"I suppose you can read human minds?" asked Bern with dour sarcasm. He was working blind, inside the computer.

"No," said Ash. "At least I never could. But I receive . . ." The computer pictures vanished from his mind, replaced by the image of Nadine as she must look if only he could see her. Curled up, beautiful, but ice, ice—

"What do I do next?" said Bern. "I honestly believe I'm doing some sort of repair in this computer!"

111

Ash wrenched himself away from his thoughts of Nadine, took a couple of deep breaths, and got back into theta to finish the job.

An hour later Bern said, "That ought to do it. I feel like hell—let's get out of here!"

Ravananda helped Bern back to the main control board where Brock still sat comatose. Bern felt his way to the right buttons, and the ship vibrated like a tuning fork at the switching.

Suddenly the control room smelled and sounded right. Ash opened his eyes. Ravananda smiled at him and bent over Brock.

Nadine groaned and Ash ran to her. She opened her eyes slowly, painfully. "I killed the ship," she whispered.

"No, no," said Ash. "We've all been sick. You'll be all right now."

"Leave me alone, Ash. I want to sleep."

"But Nadine . . . "

Ravananda interrupted. "You'd better let her have normal sleep after that catatonia. I'm going to try to rouse the captain. You'd better see how many are alive in the assembly room."

It wasn't necessary. The only two survivors burst into the control room, crying. They were both women—all the women crew members survived—an engineering assistant named Lucy Ming, reputed to be Bern's girl, and a biologist named Margot Telchev.

"Everyone else is dead," sobbed Lucy. "It was so horrible."

"I thought I was dead," said Margot. "What happened?"

"We got stuck in hyperspace," said Bern, hugging Lucy.

Margot came over to Ash. "Hyperspace can kill people?"

"Not exactly. We somehow kill ourselves—turn ourselves off—when sense data is too distorted and uncontrollable." Ash looked at Margot's red hair, thinking idly that it was a fascinating shade of deep scarlet. He felt sleepy, unwilling to do any more constructive, rational thinking. He especially didn't want to think of the dead bodies in the assembly room. He wished he could just get next to Margot's warm body—Margot? Nadine, of course. Nadine.

A jubilant Bern briefed Peter Brock, who was white and tremulous but alert after Ravananda's work. Brock glanced at Nadine, still asleep, and then at the five other survivors.

"We're all that's left," he said flatly. "We're in normal space, in a solar system with two planets that are obviously civilized. Whatever fixed the computer also oriented it to the innermost planet of the two. That's where we're going, because this ship and all of us are in no condition to attempt another hyperspace trip to get back to Earth."

Brock paused, as if realizing that perhaps he could not dictate to such a small crew. "Do you all agree?"

They did. What else could they do?

It was a fine planet, thought Ash—blue with a global ocean dotted with big and little islands as green as the greenest hills of Earth. They'd passed the outermost planet first, a cold one with heavy ice caps and only a tiny ocean near the equator. That planet had sent out ships that were joined by an even larger fleet from the water world.

"A very sophisticated navy," commented Bern. "I wish we could understand them."

The language in the various radio bands was totally incomprehensible, full of hisses, clicks, and odd sliding sounds.

"Completely inhuman, I'd say," observed Ravananda. "My hobby is languages, and what you're hearing was not designed for human throats."

"At least they aren't shooting at us," said Ash somewhat defensively, already beginning to think of these planets as his. "After all, they did help us get out of hyperspace."

"And that's pretty sophisticated communication," said Margot. "All the way into hyperspace and your mind, Ash."

Ash peered at the viewer. "I think they're surrounding the ship."

"They don't want us to go any closer to the water planet," said Brock. "We'd better stay here."

"No," said Ash, "the computer has a flight path laid in, down to that planet. Somebody wants us to go there."

They voted on it, and Ash won.

The *Venturer* slid slowly through the atmosphere, very slowly as if to give the impression of sightseeing, thought Ash. I hope they don't shoot at us.

"Oh, oh!" said Bern. "Feel that!"

"We must stop," said Brock. "That must have been a warning shot—high energy, but not enough to damage our protective field."

Ash put his arm around Margot without even thinking about it. She had her chin up defiantly, but her body melted against his.

How did one communicate with aliens, thought Ash. Why weren't there any more pictures in his mind? Could he do it only in hyperspace? He tried to reach out again, in thought.

He felt nothing. Were they touching his mind without his knowing it now? He couldn't believe that. Yet he almost hoped it were true, because if they were in his mind, surely they'd know the *Venturer* posed no threat. Why had they helped if they hadn't read his despair?

"Look at the viewer," said Margot. "Creatures flying up from the planet without wings—oh, of course, they'd have antigravity, too, if they have interplanetary ships."

"They're waving the ships back, away from the *Ven-*

turer," said Ash. Two creatures—still too far away to see what . . ."

"But they look—Ash, can't you see—"

Nadine sat up, rubbing her eyes. "I heard you talking. What's coming to meet us?"

"Come over here where you can see, Nadine."

She remained on the floor, holding her head. "Tell me."

Ash gaped at the viewer. "It looks—the long one—I'd almost swear . . ."

"Well, what?" asked Nadine. "For heaven's sake tell me! My head aches so much I can hardly move."

Ash cleared his throat. "You won't believe this—I'm not sure I do—"

"What is it?" snapped Nadine. "A little green man?"

"A big green man," said Ash.

Margot laughed delightedly. "And he has a pet!"

"A baby elephant," said Ash, rubbing his eyes in disbelief.

"Not to this biologist," said Margot. "That's a wooly mammoth!"

6

"I'll never get used to the Valosian language," groaned Ash. "My tongue is sore from wrapping it around weird sounds."

"If the Zogs and Waterones learned it from the Valosian teaching machines, it shouldn't be too hard on us," said Margot. "You actually speak it quite well, Ash. I think you're upset about something else."

They were dabbling their feet in the warm water of a little lake they'd found while walking in the Central gardens. Giant sequoias ringed the water, homes for strange birds with magnificent feathers. A Zog herd grazed placidly in the grass beyond, waving at the Terrans from time to time. Ka had gone over to speak to his relatives, so talk was less inhibited, since everyone knew that Ka reported to Lorrz.

Not that Margot cared what Ka did, thought Ash. She had obviously developed what can only be described as a female biologist's maternally scientific passion for an animal thought to be extinct and discovered to be alive, literate, and endearing. Ash was struggling with passion of a different sort, so it was hard for him to focus on his mental conflicts. He had never expected to fall out of love with Nadine so easily.

"I don't trust that Lorrz," he said finally.

"Because he's the Valosian leader or because Nadine hasn't taken her eyes off him in the week we've been here?"

"There'll be trouble if Brock comes out of his lethargy and depression enough to suspect—oh hell, Margot! There's nothing going on except Nadine's usual fascination with older men. She's obsessed with avoiding the senility of her father, so she's attracted to a man the age of Lorrz, who doesn't seem any older than Brock, but is older than Stanton Holladay."

"That's what bothers you about Lorrz?" asked Margot.

"Lorrz isn't telling the truth. He says he doesn't know who sent the diagram images to my mind so we could fix the computer. He implies it was all my imagination, but I know. I know! Something probed my mind, read the problem, sent help, but Lorrz has dismissed the idea so thoroughly that the rest of the Valosian Council isn't even interested. They're too stunned by finding themselves to be of human stock."

"With that slight addition," said Margot. "That tiny symbiotic virus in the nucleus of each Valosian cell. It must have been the virus that mutated when the Cloud radiation hit the Valosian planets thousands of years ago. It developed a chlorophyll-like effect, hence the green color, but it can use hard radiation as well as ordinary light. It must have protected the Valosians from too much radiation sickness."

"I see that Lorrz took you on a complete tour of the genetics laboratory yesterday," said Ash jealously.

"Yes, my head was still spinning from the teaching machines, but I could tell that Valosians are well aware of what's happened to them. I don't blame them for being thunderstruck to discover relatives in the first visiting hyperspace ship. What I can't figure out is when they left Earth, and how they got here. The Council seemed horrified when I told them Earth developed space technology only recently."

"That means they must have been taken from Earth," said Ash. "You said they couldn't have evolved on this planet—only the Waterones did."

"Some Valosians believe they developed civilization on another planet and then seeded both Earth and the Valosian system, but I don't believe it," said Margot. "Nothing will convince a reputable Terran biologist that human beings are not products of Terran evolution. The Valosians not only came from Earth, but brought samples of certain flora and fauna—like *Sequoia giganteum* and *sempervirens,* wooly mammoth, and saber-toothed tiger. A sophisticated technology did that collecting, and did it in the Pleistocene, all over Earth. Sabertooths were available around the La Brea tar pits in California, but not in areas where early true *Homo sapiens* was hunting wooly mammoth."

"The Valosians are definitely *Homo sapiens?*"

"I suspect they're true Cro-Magnon."

"Yet they don't have hyperspace drive in spite of knowing and using the principles of antigravity," said Ash, staring into the clear water. "I guess only a rare genius like Nadine will connect antigrav with the mathematics of hyperspace drive. If Lorrz courts her, because he wants the drive so much then, hell, we'll give it to them. They're our relatives and on the verge of dying out."

"Not as much on the verge as Terran humanity will be when Cloud radiation gets to Earth. Lorrz is experimenting to see if the protective symbiotic virus can be transferred to us."

"Here comes Ka. I wonder why the Council members won't talk to us about the Magellanic Clouds, which they call the Outer Galaxies? I wish the weather wouldn't mist up every night, so we could get a look at the clouds."

Ka arrived, running up to Margot to have his ears tickled. She was an expert at it, thought Ash, jealous again. There was no double about it—a humpy, hairy, baby wooly mammoth just beginning to show tusks was what a woman like Margot would consider adorable. Ash ran his fingers through his carroty hair, wondering if she'd think his hair and hers clash in their different shades of redness.

Ka snuffled in his trunk with pleasure. "I heard you say you wanted to see the Outer Galaxies. Hasn't anyone told you?"

"Told us what?" said Ash, as casually as possible.

"About what happened six months ago."

"Tell us, Ka."

"They went."

"Went?"

"The Outer Galaxies. Your Mag—mag—your Clouds. They disappeared. There's nothing there anymore to see."

"I'm sorry, Lorrz," Ka whimpered much later, after they'd finished the seventh welcoming banquet in a row.

"I didn't know I wasn't supposed to tell them."

"Don't worry. They'd have found out soon enough. The Council decided to wait until the strangers revealed whether or not they knew something about the disappearance, but I'm convinced Terrans come not from the Outer Galaxies, but from a planet orbiting a G-type star about two-thirds out on the spiral arm. Their computer tapes confirm this. On Earth they are only now seeing the light of the first supernovae. Besides, I can tell when a Terran is lying."

"You can read their minds?" asked Ka.

"Not exactly. They seem to have automatic mindshields like ours, but there's a psychic atmosphere I tune in on."

"I do, too," said Ka. He squirmed. "I like them, Lorrz —a lot. Don't you like them a little? Especially the dark one named Nadine? She's very beautiful."

"Yes," said Lorrz thoughtfully. "She is."

"Why don't we tell them about—about . . ."

"No. I expect you to keep my secret, Ka."

"Yes, Lorrz." Ka couldn't say why he felt like disagreeing, why he thought the Terrans ought to know what probably saved their lives. He wondered if Lorrz insisted on keeping the secret because he resented the fact that after all these years of never responding to Lorrz, the Not-God had chosen to help Terrans.

"Ka is the key!" said Ash angrily. "He'll tell us things the Valosians won't."

"You can't use that adorable baby for spying . . ."

"Stifle your hormones, Margot, and listen. You've admitted that I must have some telepathic powers, since I probably didn't imagine I heard Nadine cry for help or invent the computer repair. Then please believe that the sensations I now feel . . ."

"For Nadine?"

"Good grief! Are you jealous?"

"I thought you'd never figure that out."

An intensely biological hour later, Ash tried again. "Margot, listen. I do sense something peculiar going on. Here we are, making ourselves at home with Cro-Magnon relatives, repairing our ship, and planning a trip back to Earth with Valosian representatives on board as if the dangers of hyperspace were gone . . ."

"We survivors are practicing theta training every day."

"Not enough. Not when something can reach out into hyperspace, into my mind. What if it had been an enemy? There's too much mystery, too many unknown dangers. Sometimes, when I'm almost asleep or deep in theta meditation, I feel—something. It even has a spatial orientation—to the east, or at least where sunrise occurs on this planet."

"Shades of Mecca, Ash?"

"No, but I'd like to take an antigrav trip to other islands, trying to home in on that feeling."

Ash and Margot tried to imply that they were taking a romantic adventure trip because they were in love. It happened to be true, but Lorrz insisted that he and Ka go along, and then Nadine joined the group.

Nadine was physically well, but still affected by her hyperspace experience. She seldom talked, never laughed, and slept alone. Brock, becoming aware of her, said she was sick and stayed in the ship while the Valosian engineers, Lucy Ming and Sol Bern, did the engine and final computer repairs.

The empath, Ka, knew what the others only suspected —that Nadine Holladay wanted Lorrz as she had never wanted anyone or anything before. Ka was afraid of her.

"Why does the mammoth have to go?" asked Nadine. It was as if she'd said she didn't like empaths.

"Ka goes where I go," said Lorrz. She lifted her chin in hauteur and went to join Ash and Margot, waiting outside.

"Don't tell me what you sense," said Lorrz. "I don't want to know."

"I don't understand," said Ka plaintively. "First you said you think she's beautiful, and now you don't want me to tell you her emotions. You said you weren't going to tell the Terrans about the NotGod, but they'll probably find him now!"

Lorrz frowned. "These Terrans. I wish they had not come, even if we'll get the hyperspace drive from them. Asher Holladay is partly telepathic and stubborn. He'll find the way to the NotGod eventually, so if I don't supervise it, he'll tell the Council. I can manage Terrans better than my fellow Valosians, who have generations of fear and reverence for the NotGod locked into their past. Let us find out what happens when we go to the Sacred Grove, since Mr. Holladay insists on traveling east."

"Maybe they'll be able to Listen."

A spasm passed over the face of Lorrz. He clenched his fists. "Ka, you love me, and you also love them. Stop me from hating them if they succeed where I cannot."

7

The small island of the Sacred Grove was not close to any other, so from its pebbled beach it seemed alone in a sea as tranquil as those found on planets without moons. By long agreement, even the Waterones stayed away, and the priests had been gone since the years when Lorrz destroyed their stranglehold on Valosian technology. Only the sabertooths and the simple robots that operated their food synthesizers remained to guard the golden figure which stared endlessly from its stone pedestal.

"Lorrz," said Ash helplessly, "whatever I feel, sense, comes from this statue, but how is that possible?"

Half-grown twin saber-toothed cubs gamboled around Lorrz, who stood beside the NotGod like another tall enigma.

"Because it's not a statue," said Lorrz. "I've convinced the other Valosians that it is, ever since I overthrew the priests a hundred years ago and killed the cult of the NotGod."

"It's almost manlike," said Nadine, "with an elongated torso and head, golden eyes—is it a robot?"

"Yes, I've brought repair robots here secretly to confirm my original impression. The NotGod is indeed a robot, but injured. It's not deactivated, not dead, but is unable to communicate and move. We couldn't repair it."

"How did it communicate with me in hyperspace?" asked Ash.

"I wish I knew," said Lorrz. "Sometimes Ka can tell what it's feeling, but not formed thoughts."

"Strange, a robot with emotions. None of your others or ours are that complex," said Nadine.

Lorrz nodded. "I believe this robot came with us from our original home, yet since we came from a primitive Earth, it was not made by us."

Nadine stared into Lorrz's eyes as if searching for the truth. "Can you read its mind?"

"When it broadcast to the *Venturer*, I caught traces of the psi activity. It must have read the machinery in your ship's computer and sent diagrams of the needed repairs to the most telepathic person on board."

"It has moments of despair," said Ka, tears starting.

"Despair?" asked Margot, automatically hugging Ka.

"It is sick—psychotic," said Lorrz flatly. "Perhaps it's my fault. I came here as a boy, full of my own despair and a childish arrogance about my mental capacities. The clan of Listeners—those able to tune in telepathically to the robot's dreams—had died out. Probably because their gene pattern was too unstable, or perhaps they were like me, unable to reproduce. I believed I was another Listener. Unfortunately, I was more than that. I could not only receive, I could probe. I did so."

Ka swayed in Margot's arms. "What is it?" she asked.

"The NotGod—suffering—sense of being trapped, terrible loneliness . . ."

"Turn off, Ka, you're too young to take much of that," said Lorrz. "I added to the NotGod's suffering. When I probed, I discovered how the NotGod was originally found by Valosians. It was in a cave, apparently in a stasis field produced by a box. Men came, traced the pattern on the box and released the field. Primitive men, wearing animal skins—undoubtedly Cro-Magnon men, Dr. Telchev. The men tried to kill . . ." Lorrz stopped, face distorted by memory.

"Kill what?" asked Ash.

"I don't know," said Lorrz. "I was in the robot's mind, but its terror and fury overcame me. I lashed back, demanding that it tell me everything, and I hurt it. I could sense the robot's mind closing off still further. I've never been able to probe it again."

"Why didn't you tell the other Valosians?" asked Nadine.

"The NotGod must hold all the secrets of our beginnings, of the technology that got us here—hyperdrive as well as antigravity, since it is now clear that primitive Cro-Magnons did not originate that technology. If I told Valosians, they'd take the robot apart, and I'm sure it would die. You Terrans must keep the secret until the day when I can devise repair robots good enough to fix the NotGod or reach it again with my own mind."

Lorrz paused, staring at Asher Holladay. "Perhaps one of you will reach the robot's mind."

"You have a special relationship with the robot, Lorrz," said Ash. "Are you sure you want us to try?"

"Ash!" said Lorrz bitterly, "I am a mutated freak, a warped creature able to relate only to nonhuman intelligence with ease and pleasure. Don't expect me to welcome your relationship with the NotGod. Yet I know we must all learn what information the robot possesses. Do what you can to contact it."

As if on cue, one of the tiger cubs ran to Ash and rubbed against his thigh. Ash looked at the four faces staring at him. Ka's eyelashes fluttered hopefully, and he bounced slightly from his rear to his front feet. Margot smiled at Ash as if to say she had faith in him. Nadine's face was a chiseled mask, the velvet skin drawn tightly over the high cheekbones, her arms folded over her breasts. Lorrz looked weary, as if more conscious of the burden he was now trying to share.

"I'll try," said Ash. "Can Margot stay with me?"

"No," said Lorrz severely. "Be lonely. The NotGod is."

"Lorrz," Nadine interrupted, a false brightness in her voice. "What's written on the pedestal?"

"Mathematics, in Valosian notation. I have never understood the equations."

Nadine whirled, stretching her arms out as if to push the others toward the sea. "Let's go. Ash should start work at once, before the Council gets suspicious. I want to get back to work on that virus in the genetics lab with you, Margot."

Ka and Lorrz started first, Nadine lagging behind. Margot stayed for a moment to kiss Ash good-bye.

Nadine's silver voice broke into their embrace. "You

think you have the future ahead of you because you're young and in love. You're wrong. None of us has a future unless we find out what terrible thing is happening to the galaxies." She handed Ash a pocket transceiver. "Use this to contact Margot or to get help. Stay here alone, as Lorrz says."

Ash looked at her thoughtfully. "I suspect you've got a plan fermenting in that genius brain of yours, Nadine."

She closed her eyes for a moment. "You feel too much into others these days, Ash. I don't like it. Ka reads emotions, but you get emanations from the intelligence. Stay out of my mind!"

"That's very dramatic, but why?"

She shrugged. "Pay no attention. I'm just neurotic—a casualty of hyperspace. Perhaps it would refresh my mind to play with Valosian math." She took out a notebook and wrote down the symbols etched into the stone pedestal. "Don't tell Lorrz I'm working on this. It might activate long-dead feelings about blasphemy. Come along, Margot."

"I'll follow in a minute," said Margot. When Nadine had gone over the water, Margot turned to Ash. "What do you sense?"

"I know Nadine well. I can see it in her eyes—a dreadful plan is brewing. She means to take over—somehow."

Margot put her arms around him. "She can't. This is our story—yours and mine, darling."

"Unlikely. Stories belong to the strong, and Nadine is gathering enormous, crazy strength."

"But what about Lorrz?"

"I know he seems powerful, but don't you see that he has always, always been a victim?"

8

"Ash is not succeeding, is he?" asked Nadine.

"No more than we are," said Margot, rubbing her neck to get out the cramp. "If he stays another week in the Sacred Grove, he'll be a wreck, constantly listening and getting nothing but waves of loneliness, longing, and fear."

"So far the Valosian Council members think he's ill, in the *Venturer,* and Lorrz seems more relaxed now that he knows he can trust Terrans."

You could never tell with Nadine, thought Margot. "Can he?"

Nadine rose from her laboratory bench, stretching her lithe body. "Why not? What's he got to lose?"

"Sanity, perhaps," said Margot. Brock stayed in the ship, while Lucy and Sol were so happy to be alive and together that they were oblivious, and Ravananda spent all his time studying in the Valosian hospital. Nadine spent long hours with Lorrz that no one but Margot knew about. Did Nadine care for him, or for anything other than the preservation and extension of her own mental capacities? Nadine was obsessed with the genetics lab.

They'd made dismaying discoveries. Since Valosians had human chromosomes and genes, they ought to be interfertile with Terrans, but were not. Terran sperm died upon entering Valosian ova and vice versa, undoubtedly due to the symbiotic virus. Furthermore, no vaccine could be made of that virus which did not kill Terran cells. The Valosians were adapted, but any transfer of cells to a Terran would be fatal.

126

"We might be able to get rid of the virus in the Valosians," said Margot, "which would make them fertile with us, but would destroy their capacity to adapt to hard radiation. It's got to be us who must adapt to the virus."

Nadine, who worked long solitary hours in the lab and claimed she'd discovered a talent for microbiology, said, "I wish we'd come to Valos sooner. I might have been able to discover a prevention for my father's senility."

"Yes, the Valosians don't seem to get senile, and those who survived the last wave of radiation from the clouds, like Lorrz, are all still alive and—if they're green—show hardly any aging."

Ka burst through the doors in his customary eager gallop. "Margot!" My mother's had another baby, another empath! Please come and see my new sister."

Nadine, who had not been invited, said, "I'll stay here and wait for Lorrz."

"Testing his sperm samples?" said Margot, not innocently.

"Oh, didn't I tell you?" Nadine yawned elaborately. "The sperm samples yielded a vaccine not quite as lethal as those from other Valosians, because Lorrz is a mutant —but still lethal."

Ka tugged at Margot's Valosian tunic, and she realized he was sensing her complete disbelief.

"That's true," he said. "Lorrz told me."

"Sorry, Nadine," said Margot, chagrined.

"Don't be," said Nadine. "Yet."

The nightly mist lifted at the end of Ash's second week in the Sacred Grove. He was glad. It might be good for the redwoods, but it was getting to his sinuses.

As the last glow of the sunset died, Ash saw the great band of the Milky Way rise, more spectacular than the view from Earth, because the Valosian sun had so few nearby stars and was so far out on the rim that he could see the entire galaxy on edge. He would have to wait until almost morning before he saw the blackness where the clouds used to be. Lorrz had told him that he'd see the faint trail of dust and occasional stars that used to bridge the gaps between the Milky Way and the Magellanic Clouds, but beyond that, nothing.

He stroked a tiger cub asleep with its head in his lap, and wondered if he'd get a picture from the silent robot again. Last night, for the first time since the *Venturer* had left hyperspace, Ash had received more than vague emotions from the NotGod. He'd seen an image in his mind, a creature with wings. It was purple, and a monster.

As he stared across the darkening sky, he thought for a minute that another monster was flying toward him, but it was only Ka, hurrying to the Sacred Grove on antigrav.

"What's the matter?"

Ka was obviously upset. "You must come at once, Lorrz says. He didn't want anyone to talk about it on radio, so he sent me to get you. You're the only one who might be able to reason with Nadine."

"What's she done now?"

"She's going to have Lorrz's baby."

No one could move Nadine. She was adamant. No abortion, no hysterectomy, nothing but continuation of pregnancy, now so early that only tests indicated it and the fact that the fetus contained the symbiotic virus.

Dr. Ravananda went over the facts with Margot and Ash. Three weeks before, Nadine had tested Lorrz's sperm, finding that although it could not be injected into somatic Terran cells, it would fertilize Terran ova. The haploid ovum evidently accepted the virus, so the resulting embryo contained virus in all cells. Ravananda said Nadine ought to have a hysterectomy to cut off blood supply from the uterus, because if virus from the fetus passed into the maternal blood stream, Nadine would die.

"Virus can pass the placental barrier any time during pregnancy, particularly during labor," said Ravananda.

"I think it won't pass through at all," said Nadine.

"Your husband and I feel you should not take the risk."

Ash tried not to look at Brock, who had turned suddenly from a depressed man, brooding about his failure to guide his ship through a crisis, to a possessive husband seething with fury.

Brock turned on Lorrz. "I'd like to kill you!"

"I did nothing," said Lorrz, stony with different rage.

Nadine touched Brock condescendingly, delicately tapping her fingers on his fists. "How many times do I have to tell you that I impregnated myself with Lorrz's sperm samples in storage here from previous experiments? Ask Ka if I'm telling the truth—he's a walking lie detector."

Brock swung his heavy head to look at the mammoth. "He's Lorrz's creature."

"No," said Lorrz, his voice actively angry for the first time. "Ka loves me, but he is his own person. He will not lie to you about the emotions he senses in others."

"Nadine tells the truth," said Ka softly, "but not all the truth. There is also delight in secrecy and power . . ."

"Certainly," said Nadine with scorn. "I've made a scientific breakthrough, and when the baby is born I'll be able to use some of its blood to give all of you the Valosian virus." She leaned forward, her eyes smoldering with the intensity of her determination. "The virus in Lorrz's cells is mutant, giving him special powers and longevity surpassing that of other Valosians. During chromosome division and separation in spermatogenesis, the virus is apparently weakened, for that in sperm cells is not as lethal to humans as the virus from other body cells. I think it is further weakened when a sperm combines successfully with an ovum, causing the virus to be redistributed through the nuclei of the embryonic somatic cells."

Ka waggled his trunk, and only Ash saw Lorrz reach

out, ostensibly to pat him, but with the effect of stopping Ka from speaking. That meant, thought Ash with sudden fear, that Ka sensed something else in Nadine. What plan was she not talking about?

"That's that," said Nadine. "I'm staying pregnant and someday I'll know what you know, Lorrz, only I'll be different. I will use it!"

They turned like one to look at Lorrz, who rose slowly. Gesturing to Ka to accompany him, he walked out.

"What did all that mean?" said Ash to Nadine. He felt as if he could have spanked her.

She had never looked more beautiful. "Lorrz doesn't know how to use power fully, and I do. With the Valosian virus I could live long enough and have enough mental power to solve the mysteries of the universe."

"Nadine, you're just crazy," said Margot angrily. "I won't believe it was necessary for anyone to get pregnant as a scientific experiment. You're not enough of a biologist and you're too impatient. Lorrz, Ravananda, and I could have worked in the genetics lab to accomplish what you want—a vaccine—now that we know ovum fertilization is necessary."

"Go ahead," sneered Nadine. "In the meantime, I have things to say to Lorrz. No, Peter, don't get up. I don't want you to come with me. As far as I'm concerned, we are no longer married."

"Then you did it to get Lorrz," said Brock.

Nadine smiled, perhaps for the first time since she tried to kill the *Galactic Venturer*. "I wonder," she said.

Toward morning, when the tattered remnants of the star bridge to the vanished Outer Galaxies hung in the blackness of the Valosian night sky, Ka woke up, immediately aware that Lorrz was troubled. The baby mammoth's room in the quarters for Council members was next to that of Lorrz, so Ka pressed his ear against the wall and heard Nadine Holladay's voice, low and insistent. She was talking about the NotGod, Ka realized, a chill passing down his spine.

"Valosians won't care if we take it," said Nadine. "They haven't treated it as a god for a long time now."

"Not long enough," said Lorrz. "You forget that many of the adults on Valos can remember a time when there were priests tending the NotGod and when sacrilege was severely punished, as I know all too well."

"Then we must hurry. We'll get it on the *Venturer* in secret and leave before the Council quite expects it, if the Waterones don't tell them about our plan to take the Not-God to Earth to restore its functions. You shouldn't have told the Waterones, just because you like telepaths."

"It's hard to have secrets from the Waterones," said Lorrz, "since they live all over the planet, and have remarkably efficient communication. But they are not particularly concerned about the NotGod, which was never part of their religious tradition. This planet really belongs to the Waterones, and now that they're intelligent, their help indispensable to Valosian aquafarming, it won't be long before they're the dominant species on Valos, which is just as well. They are wise and my species seldom is. They approve of my going back to Earth with the NotGod."

"And the Council approves of you as the Valosian ambassador to Earth," said Nadine sourly. "I think they want to get rid of you, dear Lorrz."

There was silence, and Ka sensed the bitterness in his Valosian friend. Ka wondered if Lorrz had had too many years of hate. Who would Lorrz betray? Ka's young mind was trying to grapple with the problem when he heard Nadine laugh.

"At least I'll be rid of that hairy animal that goes everywhere you go," she said.

"Ka is going with us to Earth, in stasis. The Council permits it."

"I don't want him."

"I do."

Ka held his breath while waves of emotion came from Nadine. He was surprised that she was feeling more fear than dislike. It was easier for Nadine Holladay to hide feelings from herself than from Ka. He had never thought of himself as dangerous before. Then he sensed resignation in the Terran, and Lorrz won, for once.

"Oh, all right," said Nadine. "But keep your word with me about the hyperspace drive."

"Of course," said Lorrz evenly. "When our engineers complained to me that you would not let them help repair the drive part of the ship, I told them they could not possibly understand it yet. That may be true, but my mutation permits me to understand it easily. However, I do not like or trust my fellow Valosians enough to give them the drive before I've found out what Earth is like . . ."

"You mean, before you've found out what the NotGod knows."

"Yes," said Lorrz harshly. "He holds the secret of our origins."

Nadine laughed, not pleasantly. "And the secret of great power, perhaps immortality! You and I are probably very much alike, Lorrz. And I may need you. If you're less affected by hyperspace than Terrans, you may have to run the ship."

"That's why you're in my room tonight?"

"Listen to me, Lorrz!" Nadine's desperation was almost palpable. "You must do what I say. I tell you that I know a better way of curing your precious NotGod, once we get it on board."

"I think you'd better go back to your husband, Nadine. You would twist a man's mind, if you could reach it, to get what you want."

"You and I belong together," said Nadine.

"Is that the price for finding out how to help the robot?"

"Then you do believe that I know."

Lorrz paused, fear emanating from him this time. "Nadine, you've found out something about the NotGod. What?"

"No, Lorrz, first a solemn promise. You have enough integrity for that, don't you?"

"Yes."

"Then promise me that when we take the *Venturer* back to hyperspace, you'll do what I tell you."

"I can't promise that."

"You must. Remember that I'm going to give birth to your baby. I'll give it to you. Without me, you would never be able to pass on your mutation . . ."

"What do you know about the robot?"

"Are you more interested in that robot than in your child, or me?"

"Nadine, you are arguing childishly. What do you want me to do on the *Venturer*?"

"Nothing terrible, I promise you that. I must satisfy my curiosity—and fix your sick robot. The numbers . . ."

"Wait, Nadine, I sense that Ka is awake. I'll talk to you about it tomorrow. Now shut up and get into my bed."

Ka was miserable. He loved the Terrans, especially Margot, but he loved Lorrz, too. As the work on the *Venturer* progressed, and Lorrz did not tell him what he was planning with Nadine, Ka took to following Ash Holladay around. He sensed that Ash was unhappy, because he had not truly contacted the NotGod and did not dare return to the Sacred Grove because the Council was getting suspicious. Ash, in his own unhappiness, seemed to understand Ka.

"Care to tell me about it, Ka?"

"Oh, Ash, I can't. Does everyone know I'm upset?"

"It's obvious. To begin with, your ears, trunk, and tail droop. What's wrong between you and Lorrz?"

"He and Nadine . . ." Ka choked back the words.

"Everyone knows they're now living together, presumably having sex even if they don't seem to have emotional closeness. They act like enemies who've made a pact—they're planning something! Is that it, Ka?"

"I don't know what it is," said Ka. "I'm worried. It's got to do with the ship, but Lorrz won't confide in me."

Lorrz had announced that he would help run the ship, setting up light local stasis fields into which the Terrans could retreat if overcome with hyperspace sickness. Nadine had been overjoyed when preliminary trials revealed that Valosians did not get sick in hyperspace, but Ash resolved to stay awake and functioning on the trip back to Earth. If Lorrz had a mysterious plan, Ash wanted to be able to control it.

The plan outlined to the Great Council some days before had stated that the *Venturer* would leave after a month of hyperspace trials, during which other Valosians would be taught the operation of the ship. Then suddenly Nadine and Lorrz said that the ship would leave the next day, because Nadine could not stand being away from Earth any longer in her indubitably delicate condition. They seemed to be in charge of everything, thought Ash.

Ka spent the night with his mother; Nadine and Lorrz went to visit the Sacred Grove, and Ash locked his arms around the comforting warmth of Margot.

The next day, after receiving the hesitant blessings of an extremely dubious Great Council, the new crew of the *Venturer* boarded her at noon.

"It's marvelous," said Margot, unpacking in their cabin. "I'm going to show my colleagues back home a live mammoth!"

"To say nothing of a live Cro-Magnon man," said Ash. "How about showing off your new husband, too?"

"I'm glad we got Brock to marry us, darling. I love you. I wish Nadine loved Lorrz."

Ash sighed.

"Not still in love with her, a little?"

"No, I love you. But I'm afraid of Nadine—she's been too cooperative lately, promising to have a Caesarean-hysterectomy when the baby's at term—but I sense that she's planning, planning . . ."

"But she told us," said Margot. "The planning was so we can sneak the NotGod back to Earth for repairs."

"Margot, that robot communicated from normal space into hyperspace. What else can it do, perhaps once it's in hyperspace?"

"I never though of that!"

"I didn't either," he said morosely, "until early this morning when they brought it aboard in that crate. I think Lorzz would do anything to be able to contact that robot."

The warning bell rang. All seven Terrans and Lorzz were to sit in the control room during actual flight, while Ka was already in stasis in a cabin.

"Here we go," said Margot. "We'll find out now."

"By default. I told you this would turn out to be Nadine's story."

9

Ravananda realized it first, because he was standing next to the captain. He could not see, but he could hear.

"Captain Brock does not answer!" Ravananda reached out to examine, but the hands of Lorzz gently pushed him away.

"I had to give him an injection," said Lorrz. "I sensed he was going into panic again, his heart reacting . . ."

"Something's wrong with Sol!" screamed Lucy.

Ash stumbled over to Bern's seat at the navigation panel. "Bahadur, you'd better examine him. Sol's unconscious—didn't he do theta training?"

"Of course," said Lucy.

Ash opened his eyes to the visual chaos, tried to sort it out, and gave up. Lorrz was running the ship, and they were helpless—then he remembered that Nadine could run the ship.

"Nadine! Did Lorrz sedate Brock and Bern?"

"Yes," said Lorrz.

"Nadine! Why don't you answer?"

"She's busy at the control board," said Lorrz. "She can't cope with hyperspace effects and talk to you easily."

Lucy and Margot began to ask questions at once, but Lorrz stilled them with a single pithy Terran expression he had learned. Then he walked around the control room, touching each of the Terrans. The fact that his touch brought comfort made Ash feel ashamed. Ka had once told him that Lorrz had reverence for all living things and their right to live. What had Nadine persuaded him to do, and how?

"I will explain," said Lorrz. "Nadine and I are taking the ship to a place where the NotGod may be repaired. We thought you would object, although we will take the ship to Earth later."

"What place?" said Margot.

"Nadine deciphered the mathematical notations on the NotGod's pedestal. They represent hyperspace coordinates of another planet, possibly the one the NotGod comes from."

"And where is it?"

"On the rim."

"Then it's not far away," began Ash with relief. "But

you should have let all of us make the decision."

"It's the far rim," said Lorrz. "We didn't think you would agree to bypass Earth to get to a hypothetical planet almost directly across the galaxy from Valos."

"But why couldn't we go there after going to Earth?" asked Ash.

"Because I'm in no hurry to get back to my father's senility," said Nadine, her voice rasping with strain. "The vaccine won't be ready for him until the baby is born, and in the meantime, I've got to find out what the robot knows!"

"Perhaps," added Lorrz, "this new planet will be a place for Terrans to emigrate to in case the virus transfer cannot be made. Eventually this entire galaxy will suffer radiation sickness, but a planet that far away from Valos and Earth would buy time."

"Plausible arguments," said Ash, "but I suspect that you want to find the supermen who built the robot in the first place. At least Nadine does. Did you know she's hooked on supermen, Lorrz?"

"Shut up, Ash," shouted Nadine. "It's hard enough managing this ship by touch."

"Is she psychotic?" whispered Ash to Ravananda.

"Possibly."

"We should return to Earth," said Lucy Ming, "or more human deaths may result from lack of knowledge about hyperspace."

"As soon as the robot is fixed!" screamed Nadine.

"Better let me take over," said Lorrz. "I think hyperspace sickness is affecting you."

"Nonsense!"

"You don't look well, Nadine."

"Leave me alone, Lorzz, and see to it the others leave me alone. We're nearly there—I'm getting the computer signals in my earphones—and there's a marker, just as I expected. There must be a planet of intelligent beings with space flight."

Ash struggled to his feet, nauseated from anxiety. "Let's check on the robot before we leave hyperspace. It communicates through the transition zone, and if I touch it, I might be able to tell whether or not it's safe to visit that planet."

"Too late," said Nadine.

A solitary planet orbited a lonely sun, far out on the rim of the Milky Way Galaxy. Beyond lay the ocean of intergalactic space and in it swam a fuzzy, oval-shaped patch of light.

"Andromeda," said Margot breathlessly.

"M31," said Nadine, her face grayish, beaded with sweat. "Naturally we'd have an unobstructed view of the sister galaxy from this rim. We're more concerned with other satellite galaxies like the Clouds, orbiting the Milky Way, and after we fix the robot, we'll explore them to see if they're exploding, too."

"There are no radio signals from this planet," said Lorrz. "I'll go release Brock and Bern for the trip in."

Nadine stretched her arms over her head, laughed to herself and bent over the control board once more.

"Wait, Nadine!" cried Ash.

The ship sped on toward the planet, and just outside her atmosphere, it was struck by energy bolts much stronger than those from the monitors of the Valosian system. It careened in space like a small boat in a hurricane.

Lorrz ran back as Ash grabbed Nadine. With the strength of a tigress, she hurled Ash back against Lorrz and touched the controls again. The ship hurtled through the energy barrage, down, down to the surface.

Brock staggered to the board, picked Nadine up, and threw her into Lorrz's arms. "You'll never get the ship down intact yourselves, not through this!"

"Get us back into hyperspace, Peter," said Ash.

"No!" said Nadine, clawing at Lorrz to get free.

The ground rose up to meet them and Brock leveled the ship off on its antigrav, into a close orbit around the planet. He grunted with relief.

"We must be below the defensive weapons now," said Brock. "The ship took a beating, but not too badly. I think we'd better not try hyperspace again until we inspect the ship carefully. I'll keep her in orbit so we'll have time to assess the dangers of this planet."

"Take her down to a landing," ordered Nadine. She had backed against the computer, away from Lorrz, and was holding a gun.

"It's a Valosian P-gun, ejecting paralyzing rays," she said. "I'll knock all of you out and take her down myself."

"Do as she says," Lorrz told Brock. "She might be able to land the ship, but in her mental condition . . ."

"Damn you, Lorrz," said Nadine. "I'm all right, but I won't stand for delay!"

"Very well," said Brock. "Consider yourself under arrest for mutiny, Nadine." But he took the ship down.

Ash, staring at the one city they had found on a planet otherwise empty of civilization's traces, remembered that he'd received no inkling of reaction from the crated robot. Perhaps that one burst of helpful communication to the *Venturer* was the last it would ever do.

The city showed no signs of life. The largest building had an impressive tower attached, so the *Venturer* put down in a nearby bed of overgrown vegetation. It was only then that the humans realized how huge the buildings were.

"Look at the doorways," said Margot in awed tones. "Much too big for us or for the NotGod, who's about our size. We've come to the wrong planet."

Once it was determined that the air was breathable,

Nadine was the first to leave the ship, striding toward the main domed building.

"Wait, Nadine!" called Lorrz.

"You'd better tend her," said Brock heavily. "You let her get us into this. I'm going to inspect the ship with Lucy and Sol."

Ash and Margot followed Lorrz after releasing Ka. The three of them waded through tall grass, which Ka insisted on sampling with no apparent ill effects, past incredible treelike forms and magnificent flowers. Since they took a circuitous route to the building in order to examine a particularly old tree, they stumbled over the skeleton first.

"It's huge!" said Ash. "Look at that head. Reminds me of something . . ."

Margot bent over the skull. "It ought to. That's a dinosaur skeleton or I'll eat my Ph.D."

"Impossible."

"You go find out what's happening inside. I've got to look at this heap of bones. Ka, please stay—I don't want to be alone."

Ash found Lorrz and Nadine in the main room of the building, staring at five oddly shaped, enormous chairs and five portraits which hung on the walls.

"Fee, Fie, Fo, Fum," said Ash, "those are giant's chairs, and the paintings . . ."

"I don't know what they are," said Lorrz. "Do you suppose they are representations of pet monsters, or of the creatures who once ruled here?"

"I think they left a skeleton outside," said Ash. "Margot's studying it, but Nadine and I, being Terran, know what they look like, don't you Nadine?"

"Dragons. Purple dragons." She trembled with rage. "Not men at all."

"I saw a purple dragon in my mind when I was with the NotGod," said Ash. "It must have been thinking of dragons—only the one I saw had wings. These don't."

"Maybe they fold into the body or out of sight some way," said Lorrz. "Since the size of the buildings indicates a nonhuman civilization, I'll accept that these are the original inhabitants of this planet. The robot must have come from here, or have known them, but I don't see how he fits into this civilization. We must see if there are other robots."

"I want to get into that tower," said Nadine. "The entrance must be here, because there was no door to it outside."

"Over here," said Ash, "but I can't open it."

Lorrz put his long fingers against the lock and closed his eyes.

"What are you doing?" asked Ash.

"One of his many secrets," said Nadine sourly. "Another reason why I want the Valosian virus, his mutated version. When he tries, Lorrz can sense out the patterns in machinery of all kinds, especially electronic. Why do you think he caused the Valosian revolution practically single-handed, or why he thought he could cure the robot himself? Leave him alone; he'll open that lock."

A half-hour later, with the aid of some tools, the door opened into a hall that immediately lighted, showing a curving ramp at the rear.

But they could not get in.

"A stasis field, very powerful," said Lorrz. "I can't tell where it's coming from, and it won't permit entry."

At that moment Margot and Ka joined them, both excited. "There are lots of skeletons—Ka and I found them all over, hidden in the vegetation—and I'm positive they're from the Cretaceous. *Tyrannosaurus rex* to be exact, only with a pelvis altered to allow live births, and with a much bigger brain case. It can't be convergent evolution. These are Terran reptiles."

"What is she talking about?" asked Lorrz, angry and frustrated by the stasis field. The age of dinosaurs was explained to him and the portraits shown to Margot.

She looked puzzled. "That's not what they would have looked like. Vaguely similar, with scales, tails, teeth, and other reptilian characteristics, but *Tyrannosaurus rex* was a dinosaur, not a dragon."

"Dinosaurs were called dragon lizards," said Nadine.

"A dinosaur is a dinosaur," said Margot stubbornly, "and I tell you those skeletons out there don't fit these pictures. If you can tell me how animals from the Cretaceous period of Earth's history, seventy million years before the rise of man, got to a planet on the other side of the galaxy, I'll eat both my Ph.D. and those terrifying portraits."

They might have gone on arguing, but Ka began to cry. As Margot tried to cuddle him, he moaned and clung to her with his trunk.

"What is it, Ka love?" crooned Margot.

"Something bad. Alien. Don't like. Oh—want to go home!"

"Where, Ka? Tell us."

"In there." He gestured with his trunk to the door of the Tower. "Bad."

10

Sol Bern and Lucy Ming were confident they could repair the ship quickly, while Brock studied the computer readings on the planet's defensive monitor satellites. He planned to put the ship in hyperspace while low enough in the atmosphere to avoid triggering off the monitors, but if they ever wanted to return to the planet, they would have to destroy the defenses, since it was almost impossible to reenter normal space at a point as close to the ground as that permitted on liftoff.

In the meantime, Lorrz and Nadine spent hours in the main room of the "palace," as Margot dubbed the main building, trying to turn off the stasis field. Ka refused to enter the building again, but went with Margot, Ash, and Ravananda to explore the rest of the city.

"We've found food synthesizers, working and simple robots, all deactivated," reported Ash at the meeting in the Council Chamber that night. "Maybe some of them are repair robots, but they're in worse shape than ours."

The humans turned to look at the still shape of the robot called NotGod, standing where they'd placed it in the center of the mosaic floor where an alien solar system was pictured.

"There must be a way of repairing this robot," said Nadine. "Haven't you been able to listen to its mind here, Ash?"

"I thought for sure that going into hyperspace would activate it, but it feels dead to me. Do you sense anything, Lorrz?"

"No, but Ka did before we brought it in here. Ka says the robot is waiting again."

"Waiting?" asked Ash.

"Again?" said Nadine.

"That's the feeling Ka got—and that the robot is feeble. But Ka is sure that there's something alive and dreaming, behind the stasis field in the tower."

"Let's take turns probing," said Ash. "Maybe we can wake up whatever's in the field."

"Impossible," said Lorrz. "The stasis field is much too strong for any living creature to wake up. But we can still try mental probing. Now what else did you find in the city?"

"Skeletons of dinosaurs," said Margot, "in almost every building, scattered about in various rooms as if they were all performing ordinary activities—remember that these were intelligent, civilized dinosaurs—and as if they all died at once. Their machines—like microlibraries and Valosian teaching apparatus, oddly enough—are utterly useless, burned out. We'll get no information from the neodinosaur equivalent of books, but there must be some connection with Valos."

"No information," said Nadine. "Damn."

"And the skeletons have extra bones," said Margot. "I know these dinosaurs had wings."

"But they couldn't possibly have flown with that weight," objected Lucy.

"Neither can Ka without an antigrav collar, and these creatures had collars, too, identical to those from Valos."

Lorrz grimaced. "I can't believe that intelligent dinosaurs from Earth came here and went back millions of years later to pick up primitive men and turn them into Valosi."

Ash pointed to the portraits glowering from the walls. "It looks to me as if dragons found in dinosaurs creatures they could make over in their own image. Ah well, beauty is in the eye of the beholder."

"And only the robot can tell us the connection with Cro-Magnon man," said Nadine, facing the shining object as if it were now her enemy. "Sometime I'll make it tell."

But disaster hit them again. On the first orbital test flight of the repaired *Venturer,* the monitors lashed back when Brock tried to put them out of action. The *Venturer* returned to the palace grounds with its antigrav damaged, and Lucy said repairs might take a year, using metals from the city to make parts.

"When your pregnancy is at term," said Ravananda to Nadine, "I will do the Caesarean-hysterectomy, but everyone must help me set up a better operating room in the ship's medical quarters."

"Fine," said Nadine. "Now there's time to find out how dragons achieved galactic travel in an era when the remote progenitors of *Homo sapiens* were squealing little mammals trodden on by *Tyrannosaurus rex*."

"Yes," said Margot with a biologist's enthusiasm, "and why dinosaurs went on to civilization here when they died out on Earth, and why there's no animal life . . ."

"Who cares about dinosaurs," interrupted Nadine. "It's the dragons' secrets I want. Perhaps they knew about other galaxies—and perhaps they were very long-lived!"

Seven months of incredibly hard work later, the ship was almost ready, but the tower was unopened and the NotGod still stood under the dragon portraits, silent, waiting.

Ash took holograms of everything from buildings to bones, for UN records. They found fragments of writing which were typically Valosian—"a hissing sort of language you might expect reptilelike creatures to develop," said Ravananda.

"The dragons probably weren't true reptiles," said Margot, "and they must have come from another planet. They couldn't have evolved here, either."

"They came from that solar system," said Lorrz, pointing to the mosaic floor beneath the NotGod. "Does anyone have any idea where it could be?"

"No, and I can't find any convenient mathematical coordinates for normal or hyperspace," said Nadine peevishly. She was not having an easy pregnancy, yet was constantly annoyed by the solicitude the others showed her, especially since Margot was pregnant, healthy, and active. "Why did they write coordinates for this planet upon the robot's pedestal, but not for their home planet?"

"Maybe it doesn't exist any more," said Ash. "They

must have come here a long time ago. Maybe it was their sun that went supernova and killed the dinosaurs on Earth."

"Or maybe they came from the Clouds," said Nadine. "We still haven't found out what happened there. I was wrong to bring you all to this planet, clear across the galaxy. I apologize." She looked—incredibly—ready to cry.

As the others rushed to reassure Nadine that they didn't really mind, that this planet was an important discovery, and that the Magellanic Clouds actually disappeared thousands of years ago—Ash wondered. Nadine apologizing was an unusual phenomenon in itself, but however ill and irritable she was these days, she was not frightened, not eager to return to Earth. And how insane was she?

As Nadine's pregnancy approached term—one month away—Lorrz withdrew into himself more and more. He no longer lived with Nadine, who quarrelled with him constantly, and no longer seemed able or willing to share empathy with Ka, who moped and clung to Margot. Lorrz spent most of his time in the *Venturer,* studying how to run the ship—an easy process for a man with the capacity for telepathic resonance with machinery. The trip back to Earth might be hazardous, and he might be the only one able to stand it if anything went wrong. He learned to speak Terran Basic, too.

Ash began to spend many hours outside the tower door, trying to think his way past the stasis field Lorrz had given up on. He took to sitting with his back against the Not-God's golden body while he sketched the portraits or practiced theta meditation. Sometimes he drifted off into visual reverie instead, imagining what it would be like to be a parent, or how the dragons must have lolled on their five thrones or popped up out of the tower—

Now why did he think of that? He swiveled his head up to see the impassive face of the robot above him, golden eyes fixed on nothing. Odd that the robot and dragons had binocular vision, and four limbs with five digits each. Perhaps the basic bilaterally symmetrical pattern with an endoskeleton was the only feasible one for large land animals, so that convergent evolution was not so improbable after all.

Dragons. He wondered what they called themselves, and what they called the dinosaurs, and—above all—where they went. Did the dragons put the robot on Earth where the same Cro-Magnon men—who mysteriously went with the robot to Valos—had found it in a cave? Legends of dragons are found in almost every human culture. Perhaps it wasn't a coincidence.

Popped up? Out?

Ash slowly got to his feet, still in a reverie. He walked outside, turned on his antigrav, and rose slowly up the wall of the tower. He'd passed over it many times and knew it was covered with a strange domed roof designed in the concentric circles of an iris in an old-fashioned camera. Irises opened.

He alighted on the center and sat down, feeling like a frog on a lily pad, or perhaps the princess on the glass mountain, for the roof sloped away from him and seemed to be made of thick glass. He pressed his nose against it, but couldn't see in. Possibly it was polarized to prevent light from entering the tower unless wished for.

"What in the name of two planets are you doing?" A handsome green head looked over the top of the tower.

"Looking for another way in, Lorrz. How did you know I was here?"

"Ka said he sensed you were unusually excited, in the different state of consciousness you use when you're painting."

"Alpha."

"And he also said he felt something from the NotGod—an intense emotion, as if the robot were struggling to get enough energy for communication again."

"I thought I imagined a picture of dragons popping up out of the tower," said Ash doubtfully.

"Let's assume it opens," said Lorrz, coming to join Ash and feeling the glass surface carefully with his fingers. "Yes, there's a mechanism inside, but I can't get at it."

"Undo it with your mind."

"I can't yet. Maybe someday. In the meantime we'll simply crack open this tower like an eggshell. Stupid of me not to have thought of it before. I'll get the field resonator from the ship."

"We've tried to cut through the tower wall with lasers and the resonator before."

"But this top looks different on close inspection. It's undoubtedly as impervious to direct attack as the rest of the tower, but it might resonate enough to shatter."

After an hour of their working, trying to find the right frequency, the roof beneath them suddenly began to vibrate.

"That's it!" shouted Ash.

"Turn on your antigrav and hover," said Lorrz. "It might collapse at any moment."

It did not collapse. It pulverized into billions of particles which drifted slowly down into the tower. Ash and Lorrz stared inside.

"Robots!" said Ash. "Thousands, like the NotGod."

"All deactivated," said Lorrz. "No, demolished is the better word. If the roof can fall in, so can we—the stasis field doesn't come this high."

They saw why. On the floor before an inside door was a black box, reflected in the mirrorlike walls of the room.

"This box makes the stasis field," said Lorrz. "It's similar to Valosian devices, but much more powerful."

"I can't get near the door," said Ash.

"No, the field starts before it. The door must lead to a sloping corridor winding down the tight helix of the tower. Now if I can just turn off the field."

"But remember Ka's feelings—something bad in the tower!"

"I brought a P-gun with me," said Lorrz. "Besides, how else are we to find out? In a day or two we'll leave for Earth, well in time for Nadine to have her baby there, and we'll never know what's in this tower. Shall we pretend we don't know the way to get in? Leave without finding out . . ."

"Oh hell, Lorrz, you know that human beings have curiosity whether they are Valosi or Terrans. Try to turn off the field."

Lorrz put his hands on the box. "It's easy." He paused. "The being inside the tower obviously had less power than the one which used the stasis device and managed to shut the tower behind him. We shouldn't have much to fear."

There was no sound when the field was turned off. Ash cautiously opened the door and they went inside to a section containing a model of the planet and a six-foot glass case labeled TEC.

"That would fit the NotGod," said Lorrz. "Tec is the Valosi word for what you Terrans call teacher."

"A robot teacher!" said Ash. "No wonder Nadine wants to activate him so badly. Let's see the next section."

It was so dark that only Lorrz, with the minimal infrared vision provided by the Valosi virus, could get any idea of its gigantic proportions.

"There's something here," said Ash, backing out.

"I feel it, too," said Lorrz. "Alive, waiting in the dark, but worse emanations from the walls—I can't tell . . ."

"Come out," said Ash. "It makes me feel the way I did during the first moments of hyperspace only worse, much worse, with a sensation of spinning and being suffocated —Lorrz!"

He had disappeared in the darkness. Ash cursed himself for not bringing an electronic torch. "Lorrz, come back!"

Ash took a few steps forward and smelled the creature

before his skin crawled as an immense scaly hand passed over his body.

"You speak Roiiss!" The voice hissed in his ear.

"Who are you? What have you done with Lorrz?"

"Bah. Out of the way, little worms."

As Ash was shoved against the wall he saw the creature speeding through the door upward. Hearing Lorrz groan, Ash crawled along the slanting floor until he found him.

"Badly hurt?"

"Not very. I touched something in the dark, a scaly mound taller than I, rising and falling—and then I was hit."

"You must have touched its chest while it was still asleep. It woke up—and it spoke Valosi to me, calling the language something else."

"You saw it?"

"Purple, with wings, and much, much bigger than the biggest *Tyrannosaurus rex* was ever supposed to be. It must be a dragon."

"Ash! Suppose it is evil!"

As if of one mind, they turned on their antigrav units and propelled themselves up through the tower.

The purple creature had disappeared, but the crew of the *Venturer* had seen it and were assembled beside the ship.

"We'd better get armed," Ash told them. "It's not friendly, unless it eventually responds to the fact that we speak its language. Yet when I did, it seemed enraged at my presumption."

"It flew over the city," said Brock. "For all we know it's decided to wait for nightfall to attack us."

"Let's go find it," said Lorrz.

"No! No!" cried Ka, trembling. "Let's leave for Earth now!"

"I'm scared," said Margot. "It was immense . . ."

"We must stay until we find out what it knows," said

Nadine. "This is our last chance. The creature can repair its own robot for us!"

Like a monstrously designed projectile, the creature suddenly fell out of the sky upon them, hurling the group aside as it made for the *Venturer*. It was too big to get inside, so it straddled the ship like an obscene demon.

"Where is Wirzan?" it shouted.

11

Lorrz and Brock took careful aim, but even after the full charge of both P-guns, the monster merely fell off the *Venturer* and writhed on the grounds, slashing out with its tail and beating its wings. Lorrz ran into the ship and brought out a stasis device which seemed to put the creature to sleep.

"Valosian stasis boxes aren't as powerful as this," said Ash, handing Lorrz the one from the tower. But it would not work. The humans decided to take turns guarding the creature with full guns.

Lucy Ming's broken leg was pinned, and she was taken to the dinosaur house she and Sol had occupied. Sol was only bruised, Ka was badly scratched, but the main casualty was Nadine. By nightfall she was suddenly in heavy labor, and Ravananda prepared for immediate surgery.

"No," said Nadine. "I never intended to permit a hysterectomy. I want other children."

"You're in labor," said Ravananda, "and if I don't remove the uterus soon, the virus may pass the placental barrier."

"Let it. Then I'll be like Lorrz."

Arguments were useless, because the brown of Nadine's skin was already changing, as if the melanin were being destroyed and replaced by green. She would not permit anesthesia, believing that only the power of her mind could keep her alive. "I've got to stay awake until my brain adapts to the virus."

"Ash, it's so awful," said Margot, huddled against him in the assembly room while they waited through the night of Nadine's labor. Margot was five months pregnant.

He pressed her hand and kissed the top of her head. "Nadine has always been convinced she could handle anything. As the genius daughter of Stanton Holladay, she usually has. Maybe the crazy passion to get Lorrz's power will save her now."

Sol Bern limped into the room. "Your turn on watch, Ash."

"I'm going with you," said Margot.

"You're staying inside," said Ash.

I'm going with you, dammit."

Dawn finally came, suffusing the sky with color. As the monster beside the *Venturer* stirred in its sleep of paralysis, Margot went over to look closely at it.

"Now that I can see it, I'm sure," she said. "That's not a dragon, even if it is purple and not yellow brown like the dinosaur portraits in the city and much bigger than the skeletons. Perhaps some reptiles never stop growing."

"Asleep, with an antigrav collar, it still looks worse than any tyrannosaurus I ever imagined," said Ash.

"It's a tyrannosaurus, though," said Margot, "with powerful forelimbs and a bigger skull."

"I'm trying to imagine a dinosaur with the fierceness of his carnivorous ancestors and the intelligence—of a dragon?"

"Poor tyrannosaurus," said Margot inexplicably.

When the sun gleamed upon the tower in midafternoon, Ash and Margot-waited again, with Peter Brock, in the assembly room. They heard a tiny cry and soon Ravananda entered, holding a well-wrapped bundle.

"You'd better take Nadine's son," he said, handing the baby to Margot. "She's in no condition to care for him now."

"She's dying?" asked Brock.

"I don't know. Her body stood the delivery well with hardly any bleeding. The Valosians heal extraordinarily well, you know. But I can't predict the effects on Nadine's disturbed mind. The virus has invaded her brain, and if she doesn't find a way to control her nervous system, her body will stop functioning normally."

"Out! All of you, out! I want Lorrz!" Nadine swayed in the doorway, her naked body glowing with a greenish iridescence. "I can't see you, but I can find my way. I can sense you. I can't stand your minds! Get out!" Her eyes were shattered emeralds crawling with fire.

"She's blind," said Ravananda. "Go back to bed, Nadine."

She screamed, advancing upon them like an avenging angel of death. When they instinctively drew back as if from a creature irreparably alien, she swept past them into the airlock. Before they could catch her, she was outside gulping great breaths of air, hands pressed against her head.

"Lorrz!" The anguish in her voice was unbearable.

Lips thinned to a hard line, he strode to her side to take her by the shoulders.

"Lorrz, save me! My mind—I can't control . . ."

He held her close to him. "Nadine, open your mind to mine. Let me make contact, help your mind center itself. The virus is in my brain, too. Resonate with it."

She moaned and struggled to get free, but he held her fast, and for a moment she clung to him like a drowning animal.

"No! You're too afraid!" shrieked Nadine. "Get away!"

Lorrz cried out in pain and staggered back as Nadine broke loose. She ran to the stasis device and turned it off.

"Come out of paralysis, monster! Wake up! I'm learning to see—I'm going to win—you're going to tell me everything I want to know—wake up!"

For a few seconds, nothing moved, the scene like a garden of statues grouped around a fallen fiend.

Then Nadine slowly crumpled as Lorrz ran to catch her body, glowing no longer. He sank to the ground holding her in his arms, his head bent over hers.

Sol and Ash advanced cautiously, holding their guns, but the monster had not moved. Brock went to the stasis box and Ravananda came up to Lorrz.

"Is she . . ."

"Dead." Tears streaming down his face, Lorrz looked up at the baby in Margot's arms. "I couldn't make contact."

It happened so quickly that no one was prepared. Uncoiling like a predator ready to strike, the giant tyrannosaurus plucked Peter Brock from the stasis device and held him against its chest. The massive head, skull ballooned out to house the mutated brain, towered above the humans.

"Use those guns and I'll squeeze the life from this puny creature before the paralysis can take effect," said the dinosaur. "Tell me where Wirzan is."

No one could answer.

It roared in anger. "Wirzan killed my people, destroyed everything that could help me follow him, but I know where he went. I want revenge! Tell me if he is still there, for you speak Roiissan and must be his slaves sent back to destroy me."

"Who is Wirzan?" said Lorrz, placing Nadine's body gently on the ground as he stood up to face the creature.

The dinosaur hesitated, gazing speculatively at Lorrz. "You are different. I can feel the Roïiss inclusion in your mind. Only R'ya or her robot could have done that. Did Wirzan free them?"

"Perhaps," said Lorrz. "Where did Wirzan go after killing your people?"

"Hoh, I can sense your minds now, you puny worms. You know nothing, but perhaps Tec sent you to Roïissa to learn the secret of the Second Experiment. You're too late—Wirzan said he found the secret in the Tower, and then he tried to kill me so he alone could possess the galaxy. Who is the captain of your ship?"

They couldn't help the slight flickering of eyes toward what he held in his claws.

"I chose right!" The dinosaur bellowed with laughter and climbed on top of the ship, carrying Brock and the stasis device with it. Gripping the ship with legs and tail, it turned on its own antigrav and pulled the *Venturer* into the air while Brock squirmed and kicked its other hand.

"You can't survive in hyperspace," yelled Ash. "Come back!"

The dinosaur glared down at them. "In light stasis I can still control your captain and keep the outside of the ship in a protective field. Give my regards to Tec and R'ya and tell them that after I deal with that traitor, Wirzan, I might come back and let them have a galaxy of their own."

As the ship rose higher, Lorrz sprang into the air with antigrav, hurtling upward. Ash followed, in time to see the dinosaur reach down to stuff Brock into the open airlock. The captain looked hypnotized into a trance. Lorrz hoisted himself into the lock after the dinosaur's hand went back to grip the ship.

"Wait for me," shouted Ash.

"Take care of my son," said Lorrz. The airlock closed and the ship disappeared.

Ash found Ka lying on the mosiac pattern, his trunk around the NotGod.

"I ran away, from the evil. I didn't help you."

"It's all right, Ka. No one could help."

"Lorrz is gone."

"I think Lorrz wanted to go," said Ash gently.

"The NotGod is sad, sad. I felt his grief at the picture in my mind. The monster was not what he wanted to come out of the tower."

"The robot is weak," said Ash, "but I think he hears us, and perhaps we can still make mental contact. Go out to see the new baby, Ka. I'll stay here and tell the robot everything that's happened. I think we'll do that from now on."

Ka touched the still metal. "He's not an 'it' any more."

Ash settled himself at the base of the robot Tec and began to meditate.

Brock functioned like a programmed computer, putting the ship into hyperspace and setting the course. If Lorrz tried to reason with him, Brock opened his mouth and spoke with the words of the dinosaur.

"Brock will die if you try to stop the ship."

Lorrz did not want to stop the ship; he wanted to get information from the creature riding the *Venturer* through a long, long hyperspace journey. It was only when Brock's body collapsed from the strain of hyperspace that Lorrz could take over. Putting Brock in stasis, Lorrz quieted his own mind and reached out to contact the dinosaur.

"I must be your pilot now. Those without the symbiotic virus in their cells cannot function long in hyperspace."

"And who are you, who dares to speak with the mind alone?"

"My name is Lorrz."

"Do not change the course, or I will kill both of you."

"That would seriously inconvenience you," said Lorrz politely, "but as it happens, I, too, want to see where you think the creature you called Wirzan went in order to possess the galaxy."

"Then keep quiet and don't pester me with questions. You presume too much. I am your superior."

"Hubris," muttered Lorrz. It was a convenient Terran word he had learned.

"Oh, where is R'ya? I want her! I need her!" The unspoken words were faint, but Lorrz caught the intensity of grief and fear and realized that the giant reptile was crying like a human child, like the child Lorrz had left behind.

Lorrz hardly had time to think about this before the ship suddenly dropped out of hyperspace with no warning. Lorrz ran to release Brock when he saw what was happening to the instruments.

"We're in normal space, Peter, but I don't know where. I can't find any local visual referents. The ship seems out of control, plunging into a gravity field."

Brock fought with the control board, trying to get the ship out of the pull.

The dinosaur yelled in Lorrz's mind. "You have brought us to the wrong place! You changed the course I made your captain set!"

"Look further into my mind, you lunatic animal, if you think I'm lying! This was precisely the destination you had Brock program in his hypnotic trance. Look around you—we're outside our galaxy. Perhaps you can tell us where."

The Milky Way, as the Terrans called it, lay like a scintillating spiral-armed island, 150 thousand light-years away, but covering almost 50 degrees of the sky.

As the ship bucked and plunged, the dinosaur howled. "I'm in pain—take us into hyperspace for a while."

Lorrz reported the telepathic message to Peter.

"Impossible until I get free of this gravity pull," said Brock. "The instruments themselves are distorting. It will kill us, soon. Our shields aren't strong enough."

"What has happened to the satellite galaxies, the two that were here?" asked the dinosaur querulously. "Wirzan said he was going here first, although he wouldn't tell me why."

"You need a lesson in astronomy," Lorrz telepathed back. "Your Wirzan has been here and gone; you never bothered to find out how long you've been locked in that tower. The two satellite galaxies had a plague of supernovae, the radiation hitting my planet thousands of years ago, mutating the Roiiss inclusion as you call it and destroying most of our civilization. About a year and a half ago, my time, those galaxies vanished, but that was long ago in this part of the Universe."

"What is affecting the ship?"

"We're being drawn to a black hole. There must be millions of them here, the result of stellar collapse. I don't know what happened to the other matter and energy that must have spewed out with the supernovae, or to the stars that weren't big enough to contract into black holes. It's not astronomically possible for an entire galaxy to become, suddenly, an invisible collection of black holes unless somebody is able to cause irreversible contraction by combining smaller collapsed stars . . ."

"Wirzan did it!" The dinosaur shouted into Lorrz's mind. "He's stolen the power of the star clouds. Get us out of here!"

"Go into orbit, Peter," said Lorrz, "or we'll be sucked in."

"No orbit will remain steady with that gravitation,"

said Brock. "It will decay quickly—but it might buy a little time."

Using the ship's full power, he swung the *Venturer* into a lopsided orbit. "No good, Lorrz. We're swinging closer and closer to the surface, or whatever's down there."

"Then skim it and use the resulting centrifugal force to push us into hyperspace."

It seemed as if the very molecules of the ship's hull groaned with strain, and the dinosaur riding the *Venturer* screamed in agony as the overloaded instruments worked just enough to fling the ship wildly into hyperspace. The *Venturer* lay wounded in the gloom, freed of the inexorable pull, but the equally inexorable demands of hyperspace tore again at Peter Brock.

"Can't make it this time, Lorrz," he said, his hands dropping from the controls.

"I'll put you back in stasis," said Lorrz, catching Brock as the Terran fell from the pilot's chair.

"Too old," whispered Brock. "Nadine knew. She liked it, wanted to conquer age. Eighty. I'm eighty."

"Still young," said Lorrz, adjusting the stasis controls with youthful muscles aged 130, his hands gentle when he turned again to help Brock.

"Terran—too old—for hyperspace," said Brock and stopped breathing.

It was no use. Lorrz kept trying, but respiration and heartbeat would not start again. Was the dinosaur also dead?

"No, I'm still alive."

"You've killed Captain Brock."

Silence.

"Monster!"

"I didn't know he could die so easily."

Lorrz took his turn for silence, closing off his mind, finding himself thinking of the compassionate child that was Ka, perhaps the only creature Lorrz had not hurt irrevocably. The Terrans, Nadine, the NotGod had all needed Lorrz, and he had abandoned them. And his own child.

"Are you dead, too?" The words, filled with dread, touched the outer edges of his mind.

"What's your name?" said Lorrz, as casually as possible.

"Uru. I am the last of my kind."

"You have no mate, Uru?"

"R'ya. Not a real mate—but she loved me and I—I abandoned her."

"I have lost my mate, too," said Lorrz.

"My fault."

"No, she would have died whenever she gave birth to the child, because I was too afraid to permit full contact. It was my fault."

"We are both monsters?"

"Yes," said Lorrz.

"I am alone, and the universe is so big. I wish I could find my R'ya."

"I will help you, Uru. Who is R'ya?"

TOWARD
CONCLUSION

1

During the nights Tec was soothed and healed by the presence of Ka, who slept beside him in the ancient Council Chamber of the Roiiss, and whose empathy was never failing, always ready to ease Tec's anguish. Ka had come every night since Uru stole the Terran ship, thirteen years before.

During the days Tec was always included in the activities of the New Roiissans, as the humans and Ka called themselves. This was a rule instituted long ago by Asher Holladay—now in his late thirties and hoping to feel wise any day—who said that Tec was to be treated as if he were a crippled but conscious person. Which, thought Tec, was quite accurate.

They strapped an antigrav belt on Tec and took him with them, to each group discussion, each birth, on each exploratory expedition, picnic, and party. When the children were in school, which was held in the old Roiiss library found when the Tower of History was opened, Tec was there, too. He now understood Terran Basic and the Valosi version of Roiissan, and he knew all that the humans knew. He wished he knew more.

He was sane again, but he could remember nothing from his own experience before the night that a thirteen-year-old Valosi named Lorrz had come to the Sacred Grove of Valos to Listen. From his own notes found in the Roiiss laboratory, Tec knew that he was a Roiiss robot who had successfully grown the one surviving Roiiss embryo, R'ya.

That name tugged painfully at Tec's mind, but worse than not remembering who she was or what had happened to her, if he had ever known, was the certainty that he could do nothing to help himself or anyone else. He had tried again and again to break the paralysis, but his body —and memory—remained inert.

There is nothing so tiring as being passive. Tec tried to keep his mind as active as possible and wondered why he had so many of the emotional, even physical reactions of protoplasmic creatures. He suspected that he had been designed to be as much like a protoplasmic creature as possible so that he could raise and teach their young, alone if necessary. Apparently, he had.

His makers had evidently given him an inexhaustible energy supply which Lucy and Sol said might be tuned to cosmic fields or even hyperspace. Lucy speculated that Tec was the end product of a self-engineered evolution of robots, and that those unknown protoplasmic dragon-beings, the Roiiss, would not have understood his mechanisms or been able to duplicate him. Perhaps no one could. That meant Tec was utterly unique—and alone.

"I have been alive for millions of years," said Tec to himself. "Does my ability to survive mean that I will live until the collapse of the universe, when radiation increases enormously?" Now what did that remind him of?

He could not remember and felt growing panic at the thought of living endlessly, already paralyzed for longer than human beings had existed. The humans had told him that during Earth's Cretaceous period, he and R'ya had gone there, bringing back the dinosaur progenitors of the Uruun who were now, except for Uru, extinct. Tec's records outlined the long, difficult experiments in which Roiiss protoplasm from R'ya had finally been transferred to the cells of Uru. When, how, and why Cro-Magnon men from the Pleistocene age of Earth had been taken to Valos and given the same R-inclusion was not recorded.

What is the Second Experiment? thought Tec. The monstrous Uru had said Wirzan discovered the secret of it in the Tower, a secret to make Wirzan master of the galaxy. This seemed incomprehensible, since Tec's notes indicated that he thought the First Experiment was the journey of the Roiiss from the radiation-stricken Home galaxy to the Terran's Milky Way galaxy.

"And why do I feel hate when I think the name Wirzan?" Tec cursed himself for not making complete notes when he was working with R'ya on Roiissa. The name Wirzan appeared only once in the papers. Tec had written, as if to begin a line of inquiry, "must investigate Wirzan paralysis effect."

Still paralyzed. Yet he was no longer psychotic, dreaming dreams which mutant Listeners could hear. And into his shaky sanity came the powerful names of R'ya and Wirzan, coupled with a presentiment of doom which gnawed at Tec's mind as if he knew—or could know—a dreadful fact which might destroy him if he remembered it. Yet if he did not remember, doom might certainly come.

He could do nothing, not even talk to the humans or Ka. His mind's last burst of telepathic strength had been exhausted in responding to Asher Holladay's cry of help from the *Venturer,* trapped in hyperspace. Any subsequent contacts occurred only when Ka tuned in empathically or when the sensitive humans like Ash probed his thoughts.

The tragedy was that he could not even tell Ash or his foster son Jorin—the most telepathic of all—that they had to develop the probing talent of their minds, that in no other way could he convey any information to them. Ash and Jorin still believed that Tec somehow released thoughts powerful enough to contact them. It was just the other way around.

One day Ka came in alone after breakfast, as if he

needed to talk to Tec in a way that he did not permit himself at night, reserved for Tec's healing. He loomed high in the Roiiss doorway, an immense gray, shaggy shape that was full grown and very apologetic about it. Tec wondered if Ka wanted to talk about the New Roiissan meeting the night before.

It had shattered all their hopes. When the Roiiss library had been found thirteen years before, the scientific background of Sol and Lucy had seemed sufficient for understanding Roiiss engineering. Years of study, of making tools, and trying to accumulate metal had resulted in the inescapable conclusion that they would never be able to duplicate a Roiiss ship. The Roiiss method for entering hyperspace had been deleted from the library, and they could not adapt the Terran method—even if they'd had access to Terran engineering manuals—to a Roiiss ship.

Tec knew the humans did not realize that he could not remember. When he was shown Roiiss texts, they meant nothing. Only Ka seemed to sense how incapacitated Tec's mind was, and Tec had felt Ka's emotions at the meeting. No ship the humans might have built would have been large enough for Ka, so the mammoth experienced relief at finding that no one would leave Roiissa. Ka was ashamed of himself.

And something more. While Ka scratched his head thoughtfully with his trunk, Tec waited.

"We must try harder to cure you," said Ka softly. "They don't understand how difficult and painful it will be, because they don't know how far in your mind is locked. But we must try. At first I was glad that they would all have to stay here with me, but that's wrong, because I know they'll come back for me in a bigger ship as soon as possible. And then I'll be able ..." Ka paused, lowering his head until his huge tusks rested on the mosaic floor.

Tec knew that Ka was the only protoplasmic creature

on Roiissa unable to reproduce, because he had no mate. That reminded Tec of something, too, but he could not remember what.

"Never mind," said Ka, lumbering up beside Tec. "Even if we cure your paralysis, you may not know how to make the Roiiss hyperdrive for us, so our reasons for wanting to leave Roiissa are not that important. I want a mate, but I am not really lonely, and I am fortunate, because Tasha treats me like a parent and Jorin..."

Tec realized that Jorin replaced Lorrz, once worshiped by a baby mammoth, but the adult Ka no longer worshiped; he wanted to help, and Lorrz was not there to be helped. Ka had been one of the important reasons why the boy, in many ways alien to the Terrans, had grown healthy and happy, unlike Lorrz.

"I sense your understanding," said Ka gratefully, unconsciously pushing his empathic mind into Tec's.

Suddenly Tec was overwhelmed by Ka's compassion. While Ka wanted a mate more than anything else for himself, he wanted to help Tec regardless of whether or not Tec could help him.

"Is he saying anything to you, Ka?" A red-haired young girl stood in the doorway, her hand clasping the hand of a tall, dusky green boy. The children were both handsome, intelligent, and poised on the threshold of puberty.

Jorin let go and rushed up to Ka in his usual impulsive way. Ka swung him up to his back and winked at Tec.

"Tash," announced Jorin, "is afraid Tec will start talking one of these days and tell all her secrets. She comes here alone when Ash or Margot scold her or when we've had a fight."

As Tasha blushed Ka quickly handed—or trunked—her a cookie from his neck pouch. Ka always carried cookies, which he had learned how to bake in self-defense, because there had been a population explosion on Roiissa.

Tec knew it was an unthinkable crime on Earth to have

more than one child, but the isolated five New Roiissans had expanded to thirteen. First Jorin, then Tasha, followed by Lucy and Sol's twin sons born three years later. Margot then gave Tasha two brothers, six and three, and Lucy had—by everyone's consent—a set of twin daughters by Bahadur Ravananda, who was kept obstetrically busy. Margot was now pregnant again and feeling it, especially since Tasha insisted on listening to the fetal heartbeat frequently, breathlessly reporting to Ravananda as part of her training to be his medical successor. Although Tasha looked fragile, she was fond of saying that she was thin, but wiry.

Ka and Tec loved Tasha, who bubbled with joy in life, with delight in all things living, even crippled robots. She could not probe Tec's mind or hear his thoughts, but she had an empathy very much like that of Ka, who regarded her as his special child. Tec had listened many times to Tasha confide her hopes that Tec could be cured and that Ka could travel back to Valos for a mate. Perhaps all sentient beings were afflicted with ambition—for themselves or for others, and perhaps altruism was rare. Tec felt that he had once known beings with powerful ambitions and wondered if he wanted to remember what those were.

Tasha munched placidly on the cookie, having conquered the embarrassment induced by mischievous Jorin, and looked at Tec. "Nobody gets messages any more," she said. "I feel sorry for Tec."

"Be sorrier for us," said Jorin. "We need his help." Jorin was definitely another matter, a forthright egotist who seldom got embarrassed by his own or anyone else's needs. Tec liked him—who did not?—but the child of Nadine Holladay and the Valosian Lorrz held within him power sensed only by Tec and Ka. Tec had always watched Jorin carefully, perhaps too carefully, afraid all these years to permit the kind of ease in himself which he often felt when Ash meditated beside him, Ash's mind touching his lightly. If only Ash had the R-inclusion—but vaccines from Jorin's blood and sperm still destroyed Terran cells in vitro.

Tec saw that as Jorin grew with restless haste, eating constantly, asking endless questions, studying long hours in the library, he was obviously changing into an adolescent, with an adolescent's urgent need to know everything, including his own power. He often abandoned Tasha to the younger children, because he wanted to be alone to think.

Ka had often told Tec that he believed Jorin was the creature who fulfilled Tasha, and vice versa, in spite of the qualms of the adult humans at love between two children raised as siblings. Tasha and Jorin complemented each other's personalities and talents, and no matter how much Tasha grew, she would never lose sight of that relationship, because she was in touch with herself. Tec wondered what might happen if Jorin came to know and sense himself completely. It worried Tec.

Ka recalled them to the morning's task by trumpeting loudly. In a few minutes the younger children burst into the Council Chamber, squealing and scrabbling to climb on Ka's back, promptly vacated by a rather haughty Jorin, the eldest. One of the Bern boys stood on a tusk, pretending to be Tarzan of the Apes, one of the remembered ingredients of their parents' Terran culture. Since a copy of Shakespeare, a book on Terran medicine, and a history of Chinese painting were the only Terran books outside the *Galactic Venturer* the night Uru stole it, the rest of Terran culture had been conveyed through the memories of the five stranded humans. The children knew more about Roiiss history and literature than anything else.

They all went into the first section of the Tower, where Tec always felt that he was on the verge of learning the secret of the Roiiss—where the dragons had come from and where they had disappeared. Tec and Ka watched while

Tasha did most of the teaching that day, using murals in the Tower to supplement Roiiss history texts. They all had a picnic lunch, fetched from Margot by long-suffering Ka, and resumed studies.

Jorin was more restless than usual, Tec observed. He got up and down to stare at this or that picture, wandered into section two and on the top of the Tower, popping out on antigrav and coming back through the Council Chamber. Tasha was exasperated and Tec was amused, especially when Jorin came in for the fifth time, a particularly vacant look on his face indicating that he was so lost in thought that he didn't realize he'd been through and out of the Tower again.

"The return of the green man," said Tasha. "Lessons are over." The younger children left quickly but Ka, for once, did not go with them. He waggled his trunk in distress as Tasha turned to confront Jorin.

"Something's on your mind?" she asked.

"I don't know," said Jorin.

It happened often these days, and Tec knew that Tasha felt left out. But she possessed a sense of compassion that made her seem far more mature than twelve and a half.

"Want to be left alone?"

"I guess so."

"Should Ka and I take Tec back?"

Jorin shoved a hand through his thick greenish black hair. "Tec? I suppose so."

Tasha turned on Tec's antigrav belt and let him hover a few inches above the floor. Then she gently propelled him toward the down end of section one, holding fast to the little handle Ash had rigged up so that Tec could be guided with accuracy. Ka stepped carefully behind her.

As they entered the Council Chamber, Tec felt oddly defeated. He wanted to know what Jorin was brooding about. Tasha and Ka promptly sighed, both at once.

"Poor Tec," said Tasha.

Jorin bounded out of the Tower. "Wait! I want Tec."

Tasha smiled at Tec, glad for him—but why? Tec's thoughts swirled in nameless fear for the serious young boy standing before them. Then Tec saw that Tasha was smiling through a haze of tears and that Ka had draped his trunk about her thin shoulders.

"Okay, Jorin," said Tasha cheerfully. "Be good."

"Yes," said Ka.

As Ka and Tasha walked slowly toward the outside door, Jorin called after them.

"I'm all right. See you two later."

They waved back and left. What was happening? thought Tec. Meetings and partings occur all the time. What made this one significant?

Jorin stepped up to Tec and took hold of the handle, turning him toward the Tower entrance.

"They always seem to know," he whispered, more to himself than to Tec. "They sense when I'm out of sorts, and then I have to be alone to figure out what it is before I can talk to them."

Jorin took Tec back up the ramp to the first section, to the last part of it where the light grew so strong, the sense of doom so terrifying.

There on the wall the last spaceship of the Roiiss, modeled in the image of a dragon, was poised to leave the Home planet forever.

"Every time I get to this part, Tec, I think I'm going to find out a secret, but I never do. Yet it gets stronger and stronger. If only you could help! We need a ship so badly."

So that was it. Jorin was distraught from last night's meeting. He knew that Lorrz and Brock had not returned in thirteen years and were presumed dead at the hands of Uru. No ships from Earth had found them, probably because the loss of the *Galactic Venturer* taught Terrans that they could not tolerate hyperspace. Without Lorrz to guide Valosian technology, hyperspace ships had probably not been built there. The New Roiissans seemed to be stranded permanently.

It is you who must help me, thought Tec. But Jorin was so young—what was the use of hoping? Not even his father, in whom the R-inclusion ran full-strength, had removed Tec's paralysis.

Jorin shut his eyes against the strong light and deepened his breathing the way Ash had taught him. Tec waited, hoping the boy would reach out to him and not feel so alone in the strangeness of his Valosian mind. Suddenly Jorin flung his arms around Tec. He was crying.

"I love them all, especially Tasha and Margot and Ash and, of course, Ka, but they can't really understand how lonely it is when I can't talk to anyone with my mind. Maybe I'm not really able to, but it feels as if I could. Ka says that my father could talk telephathically to the Water-ones and use telepathic force to persuade Valosians to do what had to be done, but that he was lonely, too. I never felt it so much before I started to grow big, before my genitals became like a man's, and my voice got low. I don't know what to do."

Tec wanted to tell Jorin that loneliness was known by all conscious creatures who could not share and communicate fully. Loneliness was Tec's life, mitigated by the kindness and companionship offered by the New Roiissans to their helpless alien robot.

While the boy clung to Tec as if succumbing to the last bit of childhood left in him, in the presence of a trusted parent, Tec's emotive centers vibrated with grief at his own helplessness. Perhaps he had once tried to be a parent to the last Roiiss—the R'ya mentioned in the laboratory notes—and perhaps he had once been a god to the Valosians when their civilization crumbled into primitivity with the onslaught of the star disease, but Tec was no one's parent. Tec's long years of helplessness taught him that he was as much of a child as Jorin, that he and Jorin were more alike than the boy could possibly understand.

"Tec? You're lonely, too?"

The boy's mind was touching his, through the barrier. Tec tried to discipline his own thoughts.

Section two, Jorin. Section two.

He didn't know why he'd thought that, but it had welled up in his mind like an urgent message to give the boy. Intuition was not always fathomable, thought Tec.

"Section two? It's so dark and smells bad."

Section two, Jorin. They had to go there.

"Okay, Tec, if you say so.

As Jorin began to move back to take the handle again, Tec thought furiously.

Keep physical contact. You must contact.

Jorin's forehead wrinkled. "I? I'm doing it?"

There was a long pause while they stared at each other in the glare of the walls. Tec knew that Jorin was afraid.

Then Jorin moved closer once more and placed his left hand on the handle of Tec's side. His right hand went up to Tec's head, the palm firm against it. His touch was less that of a clinging child and more that of a fellow creature.

Jorin backed slowly toward the door to section two, opened it with his left hand, and turned to move Tec into the dark corridor at the same time as he himself passed through the doorway that was big enough for a Roiiss.

2

In the sick darkness of section two, Tec tried to keep his thoughts steady so the already frightened boy would not panic, because their minds touched now.

The walls of this corridor emanated a kind of diseased energy, as if the demonstration here could not be visual, as if the message could be understood only if felt. The walls themselves reached into Tec's mind as they always had, promising knowledge as soon as he permitted total contact—but with what? What secret had the Roiiss tried to build into these walls? Why was it available only to those who could allow it to penetrate?

Jorin whispered, "The Roiiss didn't want just anyone to know, did they, Tec?"

Yes, thought Tec to the boy.

"It must have been something horrible, something that drove them from their Home planet," said Jorin, trying to speak for both of them.

No, thought Tec. Doom to the Home planet and beyond.

"Maybe different kinds of doom," said Jorin, trying to follow the train of thought, his agile mind leaping ahead.

"You're right, Tec. The first danger was to the Home planet—the increasing lethal energies—represented by the bright light at the end of section one. Perhaps it's something like the radiation that swept over Valos and Veros from the Magellanic Clouds. But the worst came later, when the Roiiss tried to leave. That must be what this corridor represents."

Jorin pushed Tec deeper into the darkness, the young

hands still firm and steady in spite of the miasma seeping into the two bodies—human and robot.

"It's awful, isn't it," said Jorin, swallowing hard. "I'm the only one who can stand it at all. The Terrans stay only a minute or two and then leave, saying it represents hyperspace, because it makes them feel as sick as they get there. But you don't like it either, Tec, and you've been in hyperspace, so maybe it's not that. Maybe it's a terrible catastrophe the Roiiss had to avoid before they could get safely to this planet."

Yes, said Tec in his mind, framing the words carefully so Jorin would seem to hear them. Well thought.

They waited, and the atmosphere pressed closer. Waited —but for what?

"It pushes so," said Jorin. "Maybe I'll find out what it means if I stay a long time."

With me, said Tec. With me.

"With you, Tec."

They waited. Tec could feel the pressure mounting— in his own mind or in Jorin's? He was not sure which. Time passed, he did not know how much.

"Tec, it's too strong. Maybe we should leave."

Stay.

The murkiness seemed to intensify the longer they were there, pushing into their molecules, poisoning their bodies with incredible terror that deepened until control was almost gone. Part of the sensation seemed familiar to Tec, but he could not remember.

Suddenly it was as if they were spinning into chaos.

"I'm falling!" screamed Jorin. "Falling!"

He whirled away from Tec and the contact was broken. Jorin broke into sobs of panic, writhing on the floor.

He should have let Jorin take them both out. It was Tec's fault. Neither of them could take prolonged exposure to the emanations of that corridor while they were in a highly sensitive psi state. Helplessly, Tec listened to

Jorin descend into primitive horror and shock, while he himself felt the same sense of uncontrollable falling through unbearable isolation, change, and death.

Had the Roiiss died and been born again on the journey to Roiissa? The corridor seemed to be trying to change Tec and Jorin, trying to force upon them the awareness of what the Roiiss had gone through. It was not bearable.

Tec knew that soon his mind would shut off, and he would die, as Jorin was dying upon the corridor floor.

There were hands at Tec's feet, groping. The boy pulled himself up along Tec's body until both hands clung to Tec's head.

"I can't get out! It's trapped me! Help, help, help . . ."

Help ME, said Tec as Jorin's mind touched his.

The boy heard. "Help you? Help—helpless—we—we . . ."

His mind plunged deep into Tec's, beyond light contact, like a stricken animal running from a fire into a pool of water.

With that plunge, the barrier in Tec's mind broke.

Jorin crumpled to the floor, barely breathing. As the walls of the room seemed to close upon them in an embrace of death, Tec reached down, picked up the boy, and sped back down the corridor.

He met Asher Holladay and Ka in the Council Chamber, both trembling with anxiety. They stopped, stunned at the sight of him.

Carefully, he handed Jorin to Ka, who wound his trunk around the inert body while Ash lifted one of his foster son's limp hands.

"He's alive," said Tec, "but he will need therapy. He broke through my paralysis."

They gasped as he spoke aloud, but their eyes went back to Jorin.

"I felt pain—his—yours—I don't know which—from the Tower," wheezed Ka.

"It hit me like a bomb," said Ash, "the sense of danger, terrible, unbearable—I was alone in the laboratory and ran up here at once, met Ka coming in . . ."

"We must take him to Dr. Ravananda," said Tec. "He will see if there has been any damage. You must both sit with Jorin to heal his mind by empathy and theta contact." And I must stay away, thought Tec, for I am the one who may have destroyed him.

Then Ash Holladay did the surprising thing.

"Are you all right, Tec?" he asked.

The logical interpretations of that sentence flashed through Tec's mind. It could mean compassionate concern, as well as the other meaning—

He'd nearly killed Jorin by making him stay in section two.

"I'm all right, Ash," said Tec humbly. "I'm sane."

"We trust you," said Ash. It was an order as well as a comment.

After all, they didn't know him. They didn't know for certain what kind of thinking creature a Roiiss robot actually was.

Neither do I, for that matter, thought Tec. And I've spent millions of years trying to find out.

3

While Jorin remained unconscious, Tec stayed just outside the boy's room, trying to be available in case he was needed, but afraid that the sight of him might frighten

Jorin if he woke up. Tec sat alone and hoped.

Inside the room, Ash was on one side of Jorin's bed, Ka at the foot with his trunk draped over Jorin's legs. Tasha held his hand, her face calm in deep meditation. There was nothing wrong with Jorin physically, so they were doing what they thought might help, each in his own fashion. Tec thought about them, moved by their devotion to this changeling.

The other humans came and went, smiling and nodding at Tec as they passed, but they did not ask him questions. He had explained, as best he could, the events in the Tower, but after that they left him alone. Six hours passed.

"Tec," said Ravananda, who had gone in a half-hour before, "Jorin wishes to speak to you."

"Do you think it advisable?"

"Only you and Jorin can know that. Please come in."

The deep green of Jorin's skin seemed grayish with exhaustion, but his eyes were clear and alert, showing no fear when Tec looked down at him. Slowly, Jorin propped himself up and began to get to his feet. Tasha tried to pull him back, but he patted her on the head to make her stop. He stood up, facing Tec, almost equal to height. He would never be a child again.

"I'm ashamed that I couldn't face the threat," Jorin said. "Tell me the truth, Tec. The dark corridor tried to kill us, didn't it?"

"I don't know," said Tec, "but I think it would have destroyed our minds to stay there any longer, without understanding. Perhaps only understanding makes it possible for any creature, robot or protoplasmic, to experience the journey of the Roiiss, and survive."

"You understand it, don't you?"

"No, not yet. But Wirzan did, so we must hurry. He has had millions of years to carry out whatever the Second Experiment of the Roiiss was, and Wirzan is evil. We must find him. I will explain who he is, and I will start today to build a ship for all of us."

Jorin sat down abruptly on the bed, staring at Tec the way others were. Tec made a mental note that as long as he was going to build a ship, he might as well perform an operation on himself. He'd like a face capable of smiling.

"Please rest and eat, Jorin," said Tec. "I will talk to Lucy and Sol about the ship. It will take years, but we can succeed. Ash, tonight we must have a meeting of all adults and older children. By then Jorin should be well able to sit and listen to my history. I'm afraid it's a long one now that I'm able to remember it."

Ash nodded, smiled, and Tec caught his thought—I've been the leader; now it's your job, Tec.

Ka lumbered to his feet. "I'll come along to make sure you make plans to build a ship big enough for me." Ka's presence and affirmation would convince the humans as nothing else would that Tec was to be trusted. Ka always knew if someone's intentions were good or bad.

"But I want to hear the story now," said Jorin.

"Patience!" said Ash severely, and then he looked at Tec and smiled.

Tec's mind filled with relief. They weren't afraid of him.

His voice faltered. He'd come to the hard part. "R'ya and I were in the cave for millions of years, but she was not conscious." He stopped, reliving what it was like to spend years trying to remember and always failing.

"After the Roiiss Elders blocked your memory, you knew only your name?" asked Jorin, sitting next to Tasha on the Council Chamber floor, both of them leaning against Ka.

"Yes," said Tec. "I watched the evolution of Earth's creatures who came to the cave and found they could not enter. During a glacial age Cro-Magnon men found the cave and played with Wirzan's box until they broke the stasis field. When they almost killed R'ya, my inability to stop them nearly destroyed what was left of my mind, because if my memory told me nothing about her, my emotions still operated. The Elders never quite grasped what it meant to give a robot emotive centers."

"The Elders tried to kill your mind," said Ash, "but your emotions kept you alive. What happened to R'ya?"

She saved herself. She woke up, breathed fire at the humans, and they ran. But when she realized that I was totally out of contact and that she was alone on a primitive planet, she rounded up some of the humans and made them obey her. They must have thought of her as a god in the shape of a monster."

"The dragon legends of Earth began there, I bet," said Margot.

"Spread far," said Tec, "by R'ya's journeys around Earth using her wings and antigrav. She had the humans dig down to the ship buried under an old lake bed, and then she collected samples of animals and vegetation, as well as live humans and germplasm."

"Aha," said Ash, "when she took human beings aboard a ship shaped like a larger dragon, it must have seemed to observers that they were being eaten. Hence legends of live sacrifices to the dragon!"

"But Cro-Magnon men were a long way from the civilized Valosi," said Margot.

"There's a language teacher in the Roiiss ship," said Tec, "and R'ya taught humans to speak Roiissan very soon. She realized that many years had passed since Uru and Wirzan locked us in the cave, so she decided to establish a civilization with the only creatures available who were, fortunately, highly intelligent and adaptable. She told me constantly what she was doing—perhaps she never gave up hope that I could be cured."

"But why didn't R'ya establish civilization on Earth?

Why did she take humans to the Valosian solar system?" asked Jorin.

"She feared Wirzan would return to kill her. I've tried to give you Wirzan's history, but it's not easy to convey an impression of a ruthless being with only one passion—unlimited power. R'ya took her human colony to the rim furthest from Roiissa, where she found a solar system with two habitable planets. She built simple robots to help engineer the Valosian civilization but, just as the Elders did when they built the library here, R'ya omitted all knowledge of hyperspace travel from Valosian texts. She built them interplanetary ships based on advanced rocket principles, but not hyperdrive."

"Did she build repair robots to cure you?" asked Ash.

"Yes, but they failed, so eventually she put me on the loveliest island of Valos, because she sensed that I could see and hear. She still came every day to talk to me, proud of the achievement of her new people, the Valosi."

"Then why can't the Valosi remember her?" asked Tasha.

Tec was silent for a moment. The telling was hard, especially when he felt that his beloved R'ya was gone forever. "She didn't dare go back to Roiissa, because she thought Wirzan was there, but finally she took the Roiiss ship to explore the galaxy, finding no one of advanced intelligence and technology, except herself and the Valosi. Hyperspace travel is almost impossible for most protoplasmic creatures, as you humans found out, so R'ya determined to transfer the R-inclusion to the Valosi, whom she'd brought to Valos in stasis. She wanted them to be long-lived and able to travel in hyperspace. After many years she succeeded, and then she decided to go exploring again, this time beyond the confines of our galaxy."

"Did she go to the Clouds?" asked Sol.

"To the section of hyperspace representing the area of the Clouds, where she found pinched off areas indicating black holes—thousands of them. And then Wirzan found her."

Tec paused, astonished at the wave of hatred that swept through his brain. He'd have to do something about that, because if he ever met Wirzan again, it must be with a clear mind.

"Wirzan had learned how to contact powerfully telepathic minds even into hyperspace. R'ya, without knowing it, had become much more telepathic than she was as a child, probably through her efforts to reach my blocked mind. Wirzan was down in the Clouds, making the stars go supernova, or so he said. He lied to R'ya, saying Uru was with him as an ally.

"She returned to Valos and told me that she wanted to take us back to Roiissa, but first she must make one trip to the Clouds to persuade Uru to leave Wirzan. She was afraid of Wirzan, not for herself but for the Valosi, who would have become slaves if Wirzan found them.

"In case Wirzan won, R'ya wanted the Valosi to have no memory of her to incite Wirzan's revenge. She systematically wiped out all traces of herself in Valosian literature, and then performed the most remarkable feat of all. She called all the Valosi together—there weren't many because she was building up the gene pool mainly from sperm banks, and telepathically suppressed all memories of herself in their minds, after instructing them to continue repair efforts on me. At that time, no other creature on Valos or Veros had a memory. She said good-bye to me, promised to come back, and left. I never saw her again."

"How are you able to remember this, Tec?" asked Ravananda. "At the time she talked to you, your mind was psychotic. You didn't even know who she was."

"No, not consciously. But one advantage of being a robot is that data recording goes on with absolute efficiency no matter what the rest of the brain is doing. Even human minds record more than the human is aware of.

And you must remember that I have been sane for several years now, sorting out data in my memory banks available in the more than one hundred years since Lorrz touched my mind in the Sacred Grove. I know now that he actually started the reparative process then, without which my mind might have been completely destroyed once the memory block for prior years was broken by Jorin. When the block went, I was able to fit the hidden memories into my mind almost instantly."

"Lorrz and Jorin," said Tasha, her eyes alight. "R'ya's repair robots couldn't fix you, but her Valosi did it!"

"I didn't repair Tec on purpose," said Jorin. "I might have killed you. It scares me—what can my mind do?"

"Don't be frightened of the power of your mind," said Tec. "Remember how R'ya learned to transmute elements to defeat Wirzan the first time. Your father was afraid of his own power, because he was too alone and thought he had damaged me. You must accept that your mind is different and learn to use it."

Tec watched their faces, seeing respect and perhaps awe. He remembered suddenly the unexpected power of his own mind. Ash was remembering it, too. Tec felt unworthy of awe.

"Please," said Tec, "I, too, am only learning about my own mind's powers. Don't think of me as superior. I communicated with the *Galactic Venturer* when it was in hyperspace, but I don't know how I did it. I don't know if I can do it again. I think I can build a ship and turn off the monitors, but I don't know if I can get you people home, or if I can find Wirzan and R'ya. I have been alive for perhaps billions of your years, but for millions I was completely helpless. I feel that I've only just started, and I need your help."

Ka snorted through his trunk. "You ought to know us by now, even if we're just getting to know you."

"Yes, Tec," said Ash, his arms around Margot. "Don't

you know you can count on our help?"

"Really, Tec," chided Tasha, shaking her red hair. "Don't you know we've loved you for a long time?"

Tec could not speak. He turned from one to the other and, at last, back to Jorin.

The boy smiled. "Be our friend, Tec."

Jorin said it aloud—and also in Tec's mind.

4

Ka completely filled the control room doorway, his trunk stretched out to give Tec one of Jorin's neatly engineered molecular memory complexes for the ship's computer. The beard on Ka's jaws bobbed up and down as he cleared his throat and prepared to speak.

"Jorin's trying to speed up production. I'm walking my legs off."

Tec glanced at those massive columns and said, "That's doubtful." He turned back to the innards of the computer, but after a few seconds of work he realized Ka was still there. "Ka?"

"We'll be leaving soon, and you're upset," said Ka gently.

After seven years of unceasing labor broken only by moments of companionship with the New Roiissans and frequent meditations in section two, Tec should have been eager to leave, eager to test the *New Venturer*. Well, he was ready to get the humans back to Earth and Ka to a mate on Valos, but the fact remained that he was a failure.

"No success last night either?" asked Ka, his sympathy melting some of Tec's bitterness.

"No, I cannot probe the secret of the Roiiss as Wirzan did. I feel that if we do not learn what it was, all sentient creatures, perhaps life itself, may be doomed."

"There may be no secret," said Ka. "You've always thought section two of the Tower represents only the ancient Roiiss battle for survival on a long hyperspace journey. They must have prepared for it even before they left the Home planet by changing themselves genetically, because the minute presence of R-inclusion in the cells of Valosi and Uru rendered them immune to the hyperspace effects. However, I've always been puzzled why R'ya and the Roiiss Elders were as different as you have told us."

"Remember that the Elders must have been on Roiissa for thousands of years before R'ya was born. Perhaps the strain of living in a galaxy not one's own changes one's structure."

"It's a good thing we can go on living in our own galaxy for a long time," said Ka. Immediately he seemed to sense Tec's sadness and added, "It's your galaxy now, too."

Is it? thought Tec. What is mine? Into his mind came an image of the foster son Ash and Margot had so successfully raised. At twenty, Jorin was taller than Tec, poised, brilliant, and awash with romantic love. Except for the work on the *Venturer,* he and Tasha were inseparable, living apart from the others, worrying Ash about whether or not they were using effective birth control. No, Jorin did not belong to Tec.

Yet Tec was proud of Jorin, who could communicate telepathically with him as if they were exchanging words over a Terran phone, according to Ash. Tec and Jorin didn't have to be concerned about inadvertently probing each other's minds, because each had strong shields and, since the day of Tec's cure, no probing had been necessary. The ease of telepathy was an asset when they had to be in different places while building the ship with the aid of Sol, Lucy, and Ka.

Tec also went to meditate in section two without intense fear, because he knew he could get instant help from Jorin if he felt threatened. Jorin, however, only went occasionally and with no success at all. His mental defenses automatically went up in section two, as they had since the day he almost died there seven years before.

Tec noticed that Ka's trunk was twitching rhythmically at the tip. That meant Ka had something more difficult to talk about.

"What is it, Ka?"

"I'm worried about Tasha," said Ka gloomily.

"Why?" Tasha, Tec considered, was one of the best products of Roiissa. She had become beautiful and a skilled physician.

"Tec," said Ka, "in all these years you haven't been able to make a vaccine from Jorin's blood. The ship is almost ready to take us home to Valos and Earth, but in spite of theta training, the humans and I will be vulnerable to hyperspace."

"Don't worry, Ka, you'll travel in stasis the way you did before, and I'll only need Jorin to help run the ship in case the other humans get sick."

"Yes, I believe you and Jorin will be able to manage, and I'm as certain as you are that Jorin will be like Lorrz, immune to hyperspace. I'm worried about what Tasha might do. She doesn't want to go into stasis for the trip and is afraid she or some of the children might react badly if awake, as Nadine did."

"What do you mean, what Tasha might decide to do?"

Ka looked solemly at Tec, the nonprotoplasmic person he had helped cure. "Don't tell anyone, because I may be mistaken, but I sense that Tasha has the emotions of—of—"

From the Roiiss laboratory, Jorin interrupted with a

mental call to say that a certain component wouldn't come out right.

"Jorin needs me," Tec said to Ka. "What emotions in Tasha are you talking about?"

"I think she wants a baby," said Ka in misery. "I'm afraid she might try it."

Tec signaled telepathically to Jorin that he was too busy to come now, and would Tasha come to the ship at once.

Ka squeezed all the way into the control room and waited with Tec. Tasha came promptly, entering the room with matter-of-fact grace and assurance. Putting her hands on her slender hips, she surveyed the other two entities looking at her with concern.

"Something must be the matter," she said. "Ka's looking at me the way he used to when I'd climb up a tree beyond reach of his trunk."

"I'll be blunt," said Tec, hoping he could out-argue her. "Ka senses that you have a strong desire for pregnancy. There has always been the experimental possibility of your having Jorin's child because of the likelihood that the R-inclusion might weaken if it goes through the fertilization of an ovum . . ."

"As Nadine proved," said Tasha calmly.

"Nadine died."

"I won't."

"Tasha!" Ka was horrified.

"When we get to Earth," said Tec, "there will be surgical facilities for removing ova and running experiments. There will be little risk then, Ka."

"Listen you two," said Tasha, reaching up to caress Ka's left ear. "You both know more about me than my own parents, often more than Jorin, because sometimes love makes two people so close that they take some things for granted. Jorin knows that I feel part of him, so he can't, and doesn't imagine deliberately taking risks that might separate us. But I'm a doctor; I've studied this problem for a long time . . ."

"What does Ravananda think?" asked Ka.

"He agrees that Jorin's sperm might be used to get a Roiiss vaccine once we return to Earth, but he doesn't know I'm not waiting."

"Oh Tasha, you must not get pregnant now!" said Tec.

She shook her red hair. "Wouldn't it be better to have a full crew for the *Venturer,* awake and hyperspace immune?"

"It's not worth the risk to you," said Tec.

"And I don't want to have an ovum or two removed on Earth, producing a vaccine, and maybe a baby ectogenetically. I want to grow my own baby."

"No," said Tec and Ka, simultaneously.

"Please listen," said Tasha. I've thought it all out. I'll get pregnant here. If it seems too dangerous to extract a few cells from the placenta or even from amniotic fluid to make a vaccine, then we will travel in stasis to Earth, where I can have a Caesarean at the end of nine months, the placenta removed in such a way that blood doesn't leak across into the maternal circulation. Jorin will have his baby, and there will be plenty of placental tissue to use for making a vaccine."

Tec clamped down his mindshield and made a small gesture of appeasement to Tasha, which he hoped Ka couldn't see, but it was Ka who took the cue.

"I suppose I'd better help Jorin," Ka said, and heaving a windy sigh, stomped heavily out.

"Will Ka tell Jorin?" asked Tasha.

"No," said Tec, "since it's obvious to any faintly empathic person that you will do precisely what you please."

"I'm not trying to be selfish."

"No, I don't think you are. You have two great longings—saving the new Roiissans the pain of hyperspace and giving Jorin a relative."

"A relative!" Tasha burst into laughter. "I suppose

you're right. I love him so much that it grieves me to know he still feels alien in spite of the love of all of us."

"So that if you are pregnant when we go to Earth, he will feel differently about himself?"

"Yes, Tec. But honestly, there should be no risk if I'm careful, and the Caesarean is done properly. I'm even prepared to have a Caesarean-hysterectomy if amniotic fluid cells still give a lethal vaccine, but at least Jorin will have one child, and Earth's scientists can work on the vaccine until it's usable."

Tec considered, well aware that he was tempted and that Tasha knew it. "No, Tasha, I cannot in good conscience allow you to do this without Jorin's consent or, for that matter, without telling your parents."

"What about scientific conscience?" asked Tasha. "Are we scientists or are we not? When evidence and scientific reasoning indicate the relative safety of an important experiment that could change the universe, do we have a right . . ."

"Tasha, I'm a robot. I have a duty to protect protoplasmic creatures, even against themselves!"

" 'That's a trunkful,' as Ka would say." Tasha grinned like a naughty little girl. "You and R'ya must have sacrificed thousands of dinosaur cells and embryos in your attempt to make the Urun. R'ya started all this by turning humans into Valosi. I'm trying to finish her work, trying to bring Valosi—my Jorin—and humans together so they'll never be alien to each other again. Besides, don't you care about R'ya's plans? Undoubtedly she made the Valosi long-lived, potentially telepathic and impervious to hyperspace travel, because she knew that she needed the help of intelligent life forms. Don't you want to help your R'ya?"

It was unfair. Tec's logic wilted, and he nodded at Tasha, who promptly threw her arms around his neck.

"Dear Tec!"

"Now you must be careful!" he said, trying to control the facial expression possible since his robotic plastic surgery.

She danced out the door, ducking under the chin of the returning Ka. They could hear her singing her way back to Jorin.

Ka gave Tec another computer component. "I suppose I'll have to worry for nine months," he said. "When I got the full force of her determination, I realized it was no use. Telling the others will make it unpleasant and strain her relationship with Jorin—and—dammit, Tec—why are human beings so complicated?"

"We are all complicated," said Tec morosely as he cursed his emotive centers again.

When Tasha had another menstrual period before the ship was to be tested, she told Tec she was discouraged. He was relieved and gave her entire attention to Jorin's first baby, the ship.

Jorin and Tec fussed over each square millimeter until Sol Bern took off to join Ash and Ravananda in their massive sorting-out of Roiissan history. Jorin and Tec talked ship constantly until others shunned their company and even Ka went gardening with Margot, who said his tusks were better at turning over topsoil than the gardening robots.

Two weeks later Tec told Ka to wind his trunk around Jorin to make sure he didn't enter the ship for the first test flight. Tec had argued that you couldn't count on the safety of personal antigrav for a quick exit out an airlock, because the ship might just go above the atmosphere and then only Tec could survive.

The *New Venturer* behaved well. Jorin, fuming with impatience on the planet's surface, contacted Tec telepathically.

"Don't take it into hyperspace this trip, Tec."

"I must try," said Tec.

"If it doesn't function properly and you get stuck in hyperspace, we'll never be able to build another ship without you."

"Yes, you will, but it will work, Jorin."

The ship shimmered into hyperspace with ease. Tec had designed this hyperspace drive as a compromise between what he knew of the Roiissan ship and what he'd learned of the original *Galactic Venturer* from probing its computer banks when it was lost in hyperspace near Valos. He'd tried to take the best of both and thought he'd succeeded.

"Help. Help!"

Tec froze in the captain's chair. Was he imagining it? Thinking about Ash's cry for help, over twenty years ago, had he resurrected that same sensation of mental contact with a suffering creature?

He listened again, probing with his mind. There was nothing now. If he stayed much longer, Jorin and the others would be convinced that he'd run into trouble. He switched back to normal space.

While the New Roiissans celebrated the launching of their new ship that night, Tec stole off to the Tower to meditate. Feeling suddenly alien to his companions, he wanted to empathize with the creatures who made him.

He wandered slowly up the ramp in section one, marveling that this race of dragons should have designed a robot so much like a human being, although it was logical. The Roiiss had evolved on a highly wooded planet, developing totemistic religion in their early days. A totem pole, made from a tree, has a tendency to look stylized and elongated no mater what form is carved into it. The Roiissan robots were cylindrical and elongated in torso and legs, so that when they stood, they were more like trees than dragons, however upright the Roiiss had become during their evolution. *Homo sapiens* and Roiissan robots had remarkably similar shapes by accident, but the result was that Tec kept confusing himself with humans the more he lived with them. He was not human. Yet he was not Roiiss.

"I'm myself," he said sadly. "Whatever that is. A thinking, nonprotoplasmic creature designed to nurture, guide, and protect living things. I suppose that even includes myself, or why should I have wanted to stay alive all those millions of years of imprisonment? But I've built the humans a ship. What or who would not need me now?"

Then he thought about the cry of help he'd heard in hyperspace. Suppose it had not been his imagination?

He opened the door to section two and went into the darkness. As the years had gone by, section two did not seem so terrifying. It was as if he'd experienced the worst it had to offer, and yet he could not fathom the secret as Wirzan had done! Or had Wirzan simply guessed the secret of surviving—possibly controlling—aspects of hyperspace?

The corridor atmosphere pressed upon him, its silently terrifying mood penetrating his brain components. He ignored it and concentrated on his own mind. Had he or had he not heard a cry for help? It was there in his memory bank, no doubt, probably labeled POSSIBLY IMAGINARY. He let himself sink into the center of his own mind as if it were a calm pool, going past the doubts and fears into the certainty of pure experience. He had heard the cry. It was real, not imaginary.

Tec swam up to full consciousness abruptly, suddenly aware that he had almost caught something else. The message of the corridor—it spoke only to the inmost mind. Should he try again?

"Tec! Are you all right?"

Jorin opened the door, with Ka silhouetted beside him against the glaring light of the end of section one. "It was looking for you telepathically when I caught something—

something—I don't know what."

"Something alien," said Ka matter-of-factly. "Dangerous."

Tec rose to meet them and said nothing until they were down in the Council Chamber. Then he turned, a sad smile on his mobile face.

"I'm sorry, my friends. You forget. I am alien."

5

The new ship gleamed in Roiissan sunlight, a work of love and art, thought Tec. If this second test flight went well, all the New Roiissans would leave within the week, even Ka, who had become Tasha's large gray shadow. Tec ignored him and concentrated on preparing Jorin for the flight, one week after the first test. He assured everyone that the *New Venturer* could travel to Earth and Valos, and back to Roiissa, piloted only by himself and Jorin if necessary.

Tec and Jorin left early one morning, as dawn touched the Tower of History. The ship rose to meet the sunlight, moving steadily into the upper atmosphere. Jorin stared at the viewer.

"I can see the entire planet. I didn't know it would be this beautiful."

"Soon you'll see the worlds of your mother and father," said Tec, thinking sadly of Earth and Valos, where R'ya had been.

Where was she now? Would Wirzan's ambitions ultimately destroy those planets—the civilization of one marked by dragon legends, the other created by a dragon herself?

"Let's go into hyperspace now," said Jorin impatiently, "and find out if I've inherited my father's resistance to it."

He had. The queasiness passed quickly and his senses adjusted to the new order of data with little difficulty.

"R'ya had similar reactions," said Tec. "Your Roiiss inclusion works."

"Then maybe my father is still alive even after all these years."

Tec turned to look at Jorin carefully. "You have hopes of meeting him?"

"Yes. Never admitted it. After all, he didn't save my mother."

"Maybe she couldn't let him."

"What do you mean?"

"I only know what the others, especially Ash, have told me. Nadine Holladay was a strange, headstrong, and lonely person who found it hard to reveal her thoughts and feelings to anyone; Lorrz was very much the same, isolated in his own mind, except that he was more damaged and for much longer."

"Am I like that?"

Tec laughed. "Are you?"

The boy had no chance to answer, because Tec whirled out of the captain's seat to the center of the control room. Staring into nothing, Tec's mind reeled with the force of telepathic contact sent through hyperspace.

"Help. Help!"

"What is it, Tec?"

Tec could not answer at first. "R'ya. It must be R'ya. She needs me. We have to go at once . . ."

"Go? Go where?"

Tec put his hands to his head. "I don't know—far away—it must be very far—R'ya—"

Jorin slid into the captain's seat and took hold of the

controls. "I'm taking the ship back, Tec. We can't go anywhere far away without the others."

"R'ya?"

The contact broke as the ship spun into normal space and Tec stared at Jorin.

"But I may not find the contact again. Go back."

The ship-to-surface visiphone activated. Ash Holladay's frightened face looked out of the screen. "You must come back at once. Tasha . . ." his voice broke.

"What's happened!" yelled Jorin as Tec pushed him out of the way and took over.

"She's sick. Ravananda says she's got the Roiiss inclusion in her blood stream."

"We're coming, Ash," said Tec, taking the ship down.

"But how, how?" asked Jorin.

"Within a week after conception, the embryo implants in the uterine wall. Transfer of R-inclusion could take place then, but we never thought of that. I'm sorry, Jorin."

Jorin knelt at Tasha's bedside, his arms around her body which glowed with an eerie green light. Tec waited in a corner. Her parents and Ravananda were nearby. Her eyes were closed because she could see nothing but green iridescence.

"Jorin?" She had not spoken for a half-hour, since her skin began turning green.

"I'm here."

"Jorin!" Tasha screamed, starting up in bed, flailing her arms. "I need you! Where are you? Jorin!"

"She can't detect normal sounds," said Tec. "You must contact her mind directly, Jorin."

Jorin nodded, climbed on the bed, and pulled Tasha over so that her body lay against the length of his.

"Perhaps she can recognize you by touch," said Tec, "the way Terrans functioned in hyperspace." It was as if only he and Jorin and Tasha were in the room.

Jorin took Tasha's right hand and pressed it upon his own face. She shrank back at first, then began to feel his features carefully until her face suddenly relaxed and some of the tension went out of her body.

"Tash," said Jorin, "let me in. It's always been you and me. We know each other."

Tec didn't think Tasha could hear him, but it didn't matter. Jorin was mainly trying to convince himself that entering the mind of another protoplasmic creature would not harm it. Everything was up to Jorin.

The boy lifted the limp body of the girl and wound his legs and arms around her. He shut his eyes and nuzzled her cheek like a loving animal. She sighed and put her arms around him. He kissed her, and their faces changed. With eyes still closed, their young features smoothed out, first into a look of peace, then into joy. They smiled.

Tec moved forward and tapped Ash, Margot, and Ravananda. "Let's go now. Jorin can handle it."

Twenty-four hours later Tec and Ravananda had their vaccine.

But what was happening in hyperspace? thought Tec.

The other Terrans took the vaccine easily. The phase of blindness and partial insanity did not occur, although they felt hot and uncomfortable for a couple of hours until the skin iridescence died down to a faded version of standard Valosi green.

No one achieved the intensity and completeness of telepathic communion available to Jorin and Tasha, but now everyone could send and receive telepathic messages, except for children under puberty who nevertheless took the vaccine most easily.

Tec wanted to get back to hyperspace, but he let the New Roiissans pack up to leave their foster planet, and at last they were ready to go. The children cried over leaving home and were bundled into the nursery on board ship, to be watched over by Margot, whose three-year-old was the youngest.

The best surprise was Ka, who did not have to go into stasis, because a pure infusion of weakened R-inclusion, minus any human contaminants, had succeeded in turning him into the only green mammoth alive. He was a superb telepath almost at once, able to report instantly to Tec on any event before the others could marshal their thoughts and exert the necessary mental effort.

"You're in a hurry to get into hyperspace," said Ka in the galley telepathically to Tec in the control room. "Want to tell me why?"

Tec told him, grateful that Ka was too polite to try probing for the information after his long distance empathy had alerted him.

"You should have told the others, Tec. We'd have hurried faster and been in hyperspace by now."

"But you see, Ka, I'm not sure it is R'ya. Suppose it is Wirzan, a being capable of trying to lure anyone to destruction, especially someone he hates as much as he does me. R'ya went to Wirzan in the Magellanic Clouds. I find it hard to believe that she could have escaped him."

"You love R'ya."

"I did."

Ka was silent, and Tec broke off contact before the mammoth could make an empathic comment. Past tense?

Tec made one low orbit around Roiissa, swooping down over the city built by robots, dead a hundred million years, for the Roiiss Elders, dead—how long? Perhaps Margot's vegetable gardens would last until other green humans came back to explore the Tower of History.

The Tower! Tec locked the ship on its antigrav, directly over the Tower, whose broken top gaped below them. The three humans in the control room—Sol, Ash, and Jorin—turned questioningly.

"What's wrong, Tec?"

"Section two. I've got to stop being afraid of it. Maybe my last chance. I will come back."

He ran to the airlock, opened it, and propelled himself out and down to the Tower, down past the shattered robot bodies, many of which he'd dissected to add Roiissan metal to the *New Venturer,* past the glass stasis case in which the Elders had transported him from the Home planet, down into the murk of section two.

He achieved deep meditation almost at once, without trying, or because he did not try. Slowly, slowly, he let his mind go into the walls of the corridor.

He was not afraid this time. He would be rescued and healed, if necessary, by minds that loved him. He was the only one of his kind in the universe, but he was not alone, and he was strong enough, sure enough of his own powers to face whatever the Roiiss had intended for thinking creatures to learn from section two.

Yet he did not try to think. He tried only to let himself experience. Some of it was suddenly familiar. It went way back, to his first journey with R'ya. He did not try to figure it out, but sank deeper into his feelings. He was now part of the Roiiss, as only their creature—or a master robot like Wirzan—could ever let himself be. No others could fathom the experience of the Roiiss, for they were protoplasmic creatures who became something utterly alien, never again able to join with other protoplasmic creatures either in their original home, if it had survived, or in their new one. Only a nonprotoplasmic mind like his own could fully experience, without help, what had happened to the Roiiss.

And suddenly, deep in his trance, Tec knew what the First Experiment really was. The audacity of it overwhelmed him, yet he felt humble and respectful toward his former masters—those sad, lonely dragons who had evolved, like humans, from primitive forms on a now long-dead planet, to protoplasmic immortals of the highest technological achievement. They dared to make an incredible journey to survive—everything.

And they dared even more—they planned the Second Experiment.

They made only one major mistake. In attempting to think of all contingencies, including their own possible nonsurvival, they had had Tec constructed, and they intrusted the care of Roiiss embryos to him. If they had destroyed him and the embryos once they knew they had completed the First Experiment, then Tec would not have met Wirzan, bringing destruction to the Roiiss.

But perhaps the Roiiss were doomed anyway. Planning, preparing for the Second Experiment—more audacious than the First—had weakened them so much that they were forced to flee from Wirzan. Tec knew that Wirzan would stop at nothing to carry out the Second Experiment for himself; he had even blown up his own sun to get energy for hyperspace travel. Humanity would be in the same position as the hapless natives of Wirzan's planet if Tec could not stop him—and even now it might be too late!

Tec roused himself and soared up the ramp to the top of the Tower once more. He flew up to the *Venturer*, entered the airlock, and dashed to the control room.

"Hey Tec," said Sol, "did you do anything? Something's funny with the computer. It started to react as if it had been contacted by a telepath."

"I did nothing," said Tec, dread filling his mind. Wirzan? So soon?

"Tec, you old hunk of metal!"

At first he thought the mind touch was Ka's, but then he realized that it came from outside the ship.

"Listen, Tec, are those damn monitors still on?"

Tec turned to the others.

"We have company. Uru is in the *Galactic Venturer*, outside Roiissa's sun."

6

"Is the *New Venturer* faster and more powerful than the old one?" asked Ash.

"Yes," said Tec. "We can get away from Uru, especially if we enter hyperspace."

"But he might still have Lorrz with him," said Jorin.

"And Peter Brock," said Sol, "although I don't see how the captain could have survived a long trip in hyperspace when he almost died in the two short trips we made to Valos and Roiissa."

"Perhaps Uru is the one who cried for help when you and I were in hyperspace last time," said Jorin.

Tec thought then said, "I don't know. During the last few minutes I've been trying to contact Uru, but he's got a mindshield up. After what he did to us, he may not trust us, or perhaps he had the mental strength only for that one contact. Telepathy was never easy for him, and this is long distance."

"Then we'll have to go meet the ship and find out about Uru—and Lorrz," said Jorin firmly.

"Agreed?" asked Tec. The others nodded and Tec took the controls, driving the *New Venturer* away from the gravitational field of Roiissa, toward that other ship waiting in space. The *Galactic Venturer* grew larger in the viewer, and Tec could see Uru encased in a stasis film on top. Tec sensed that it was a crippled ship and reached out again to the dinosaur.

"I'm sorry," said Tec after a minute, turning to the

humans. "Your Captain Brock died from hyperspace effects."

"And Lorrz?" asked Jorin.

"Listen with your mind, Jorin," said Tec.

"Lorrz!" Jorin smiled. "He's alive and wants to know who I am."

"Tell him," said Tec, watching Jorin's eyes close as the stories of father and son unfolded in intense telepathic linkage. Then Tec saw the dinosaur in the viewer lick his lips and hunch his ungainly body closer to the ship's hull.

"Let's go back to Roiissa, Tec," croaked Uru. "It's cramped up here, and I want to stretch my legs and tail on a planet for a few hours. Besides, this ship is dying."

Ka's bulk swayed in the entrance to the control room. "You sent for me, Tec?"

"Yes, Ka. I must be certain. Come into my mind and contact Uru with me. I want to know what he's like now."

They went together, quickly and smoothly.

Uru snarled. "Finding out if I'm still a monster?"

"He's not," said Ka.

"That's what I thought," said Tec.

"Let Lorrz get this hulk down," said Uru, "before it blows up and wastes a good cure."

They had dinner once more on Roiissa, the food synthesizer working overtime for Uru, while Margot showed off her vegetables and Jorin showed off Tasha to Lorrz.

Tec saw that Lorrz's customary aplomb was shattered by the knowledge that he was father to a twenty-year-old man and was to be a grandfather in a few months, when it seemed to Lorrz and Uru that only a few weeks had passed since they left Roiissa.

Tec understood when he found that the *Galactic Venturer* had run into trouble near the black holes of the now starless Magellanic Clouds, finally emerging into the Milky Way galaxy able only to limp back to the planet last programmed into the damaged computer.

"You're lucky you missed only twenty years," said Tec to Lorrz, "instead of the thousands R'ya and I skipped when we encountered a black hole, but we ran our ship through the hole's edge. You used the best method of escape, letting centrifugal force push you into hyperspace."

He was about to explain to all of them what the Roiiss Elders had done with black holes, when the New Roiissans shut him up with a plea for one last day of pleasure showing Uru and Lorrz how they had lived for twenty years.

They are all so happy and united, thought Tec. They feel so sure of themselves as fully conscious, telepathic, and hyperspace-immune. And I feel worse with every moment that passes. Where is Wirzan?

Finally he went to find Uru, because Uru might still want to find R'ya. The dinosaur was lolling full-length in the Council Chamber of the old Roiiss while the children of the New Roiiss slid down his stomach, and he grandly answered the questions of Margot, Ash, and Ka.

"Uru, please come with me for a moment," said Tec.

The big-brained tyrannosaurus rolled carefully over as the children squealed, and Ka shooed them out of the way. "Now?"

"Now." Something like angry despair emerged with the word, and Ka looked sharply at Tec.

Uru sighed, but got up and flapped his wings once. If Uru paid such attention to the voice of authority, Lorrz must have wrought enormous changes in a short time, thought Tec.

Ka's thought, as always, touched Tec's mind with considerate gentleness. "You are upset, Tec. Can I help?"

"I don't know," telepathed Tec and shut Ka out. To his shame, he found that he wanted to hit Uru with section two. He wanted to get back into hyperspace.

In determined silence, Tec led Uru into section two and closed the door.

"I don't want to be in here," cried Uru. "This is where

Wirzan put me in deep stasis when he couldn't kill me through the field I used as a defense. It's an awful place."

"No, not completely," said Tec remorselessly. "It's very instructive."

Uru moaned. "I hate it! I can't learn anything here."

"Listen carefully, Uru. If you didn't find R'ya and Wirzan in the Cloud area, then they have gone elsewhere, because I believe that one of them contacted me recently. When I was trying out our ship in hyperspace, I heard a cry for help."

To Tec's surprise, Uru promptly shook himself.

"R'ya? If she needs help, we must go at once. I've never forgiven myself for leaving her on Earth."

"It might have been Wirzan I heard," said Tec.

"I'll kill him if I find him."

"First you'd better understand what Wirzan found in this section—the secret of the First and Second Experiments."

"How? I always feel I'll go crazy if I stay conscious in here."

"Lorrz has taught you to be a better telepath, Uru. Come with me, in my mind, and I'll let you experience what I've found."

"I want Lorrz," said Uru stubbornly. "I've always been afraid of you, Tec. You were made by the Roiiss, you know. You're their creature and completely alien to the rest of us, all from Earth one way or another."

"That is true," said Tec, suddenly feeling again the anguish of total aloneness. "I am alien, and perhaps you are right not to trust me. I don't even trust myself or I wouldn't need to share this with you. I haven't had time to tell the others yet, but I think Ka knows."

"I've sent for Lorrz," said Uru, sitting down heavily in the dark.

In a few seconds, the door at the lower end of the ramp opened and Lorrz entered with Ka. "Uru explained telepathically what you want to do, Tec. He and I have been through much together, and we trust each other now. It's odd. My genes exist in Jorin and in his unborn child, and my R-inclusion has been passed to all the Terrans here, but I still feel most at home with Uru and Ka. I suppose I always will."

"You might try including me on the list," said Tec with more sarcasm than he intended, because the mysterious anxiety in him was still growing.

"That's why I'm here," said Lorrz. "I feel that you are strong now. I hurt your mind once, but I won't again."

"Join me," said Tec, abandoning his anger at the way these Terran-derived creatures were delaying him, letting himself go deep into meditation again. "Experience with me."

When they emerged from the Tower much later, Uru's wings looked wilted, Ka's trunk was limp, and Lorrz's mouth was taut.

"NotGod," said Lorrz softly, "I'm scared. What are we going to find when we catch up to Wirzan?"

"Not the beginning of the end, I hope," said Tec.

7

The *New Venturer* floated in the long silence of hyperspace, waiting for directions from the one intelligence capable of plotting its course.

Tec felt like giving up. He had probed telepathically, again and again, receiving no answer.

"Perhaps what you heard during the test flight was a

recorded distress call from Wirzan, designed to lure you to him, if you ever achieved space travel again," said Lorrz. "I think I may have heard one on the way to Roiissa. Did you, Uru?"

The gigantic dinosaur, riding in a bubble on top of the *New Venturer* as he had for so long in the old ship, grumbled, "I'm not that good a telepath. Maybe I did, but thought I was imagining it. How are we going to find out if it's Wirzan?"

"What is it, Ka?" asked Tec.

He twitched his ears and coiled his trunk as if to emphasize a point. "I haven't been listening to your mind, Tec, but when you talk about that call you heard, I can't help noticing that you react emotionally in a way you wouldn't if you had tuned in to an enemy."

"React, react, what are you talking about?" snorted Uru, obviously jealous of the place Ka had in New Roiissan hearts.

"Ka knows," said Ash. "His emphatic insight is usually more reliable than what we deduce intellectually from insufficient data."

"Wait!" said Tec. He probed again. "Where, where?"

"This way, this way. Help, help."

Had he heard it? Had he sensed the directions? Tec checked his memory centers for confirmation of the reality of the message. It was real, but the more he tried to pin down the direction consciously, the more it escaped him.

"I'm losing the direction!"

A hairy green trunk pushed him back to face the ship's controls. "Don't think," said Ka softly. "Put your hands on the controls and go where it seems right to you."

"Yes," said Tec. "Ka, Jorin, Lorrz, Ash! Go into theta and help me."

Slowly, slowly Tec felt his way through hyperspace, the ship gliding like a phantom fish in a forgotten sea.

An enormous pinched-off area loomed ahead. Tec came

out of his trance to stare unbelievingly at the computer's matter-of-fact assessment of the ship's whereabouts.

"We've left the area of hyperspace belonging to the Milky Way galaxy," he said. "This is the neighboring spiral galaxy, that Terrans call M31."

"On Earth it's seen as the great galaxy in the constellation Andromeda," said Ash, "the only thing outside your own galaxy visible to the naked eye from Earth. Do you think the distress calls come from this galaxy?"

"I'm certain, now," said Tec. "Wirzan must be here and very powerful, judging from the size of that black hole. In the lifetime of a star, nuclear burning uses up only a small amount of the star's energy, but when it collapses with supernovae formation, fifty percent of the mass-energy is made available. Wirzan has used up the Magellanic Clouds and he's starting on M31. The core is one huge black hole now."

"Well, what are we waiting for?" thundered Uru. "Let's get out of hyperspace and kill him!"

Tec had never killed a sentient being, but all agreed that Wirzan must be found and stopped. What was the use of returning to Earth or Valos if Wirzan went on destroying? And what if R'ya were still alive as Wirzan's prisoner?

He opened his mind to all the others. "My decision is to leave hyperspace and investigate M31. If Wirzan is there, destroying this galaxy as he probably destroyed the Magellanic Clouds, then we must stop him. Do you agree?"

They agreed.

Then Tec found that he could not enter normal universal space from that area of hyperspace. The ship would not obey.

"Why are we still in hyperspace?" said Lorrz.

Tec wrestled with the controls. "A huge force is preventing entry. When the ship tries to leave hyperspace, something takes over control of the ship's computer. Only Wirzan could do that!"

"Then we're blocked," cried Ash.

"Try, try." The faint telepathic message caressed Tec's mind. Wirzan surely would not be so illogical as to seduce with words while rejecting entry. Tec's ambivalence vanished as he committed himself fully to his course of action. Even his emotive centers stopped vibrating so uncomfortably.

"Friends," he said to the crew of the *New Venturer,* "someone needs our help against Wirzan. If not R'ya, then other sentient beings. We must take over mental control of our computer from Wirzan during the transition from hyper to normal space in M31. Take the controls, Lorrz. Ka, Jorin—help me with the computer."

Tec touched the computer with both hands, pausing for a moment to rest in the eerie peace of hyperspace, his mind gathering strength. He could feel the minds of the others, doing their jobs, waiting for his entry into battle. The children in the back of the ship were soothed by Margot, Tasha, and Ravananda. Lucy, Sol, and Ash remained unobtrusively on the alert and ready to help at one side of the control room. Ka's mind was like a quiet pool, ready to cleanse and calm any suffering. Even Uru, uncomfortable in his bubble overhead, seemed to be building a savage but majestic intensity of emotion and determination tempered by intelligence unknown to his reptilian ancestors.

"I want to find R'ya," said Uru. "Take us in, Tec."

Into galactic space, a galaxy not their own. Tec fought with the entity trying to possess the ship, trying to kill Tec's mind in a war raging silently in the computer.

"We may have a chance," muttered Tec. "He's being distracted."

"What?" asked Jorin.

"Hush," said Ka. "Let Tec intuit what he can."

Fighting for entry, Tec could feel only agony as they

tried to make the journey out of hyperspace, but the pain was shared. The enemy might have other enemies, but would the *New Venturer* emerge only into a trap?

"Trapped, trapped—help, help!"

The cry pierced Tec's mind like a desperate call across dark millennia. Perhaps it was. Whatever trap existed, they must enter it.

Mentally wrenching control of the computer away from the enemy, Tec became the ship. He forced his way into the barrier, the hull shuddering with strain, bearing his precious cargo of protoplasmic creatures to M31 and the ugly flowering of the Second Experiment.

A few stars appeared in the viewer as Tec gave the ship back to itself, the control of the computer still his. The entire area around them was thick with cosmic dust and vision was poor. They had won—a chance at unimaginable danger?

They could not see, but the ship could. Deep in the murk ahead of them was another battle.

"Wirzan," said Tec, his fingers and mind trying to read the ship. "It must be Wirzan in there."

"But what's happening?" said Jorin.

Lorrz looked over at Tec out of long years of suffering, as if he could understand Tec because, robot and man, they were very much alike. Each had been alien for a lifetime.

"The final enemy?" asked Lorrz ironically.

The final enemy was within, thought Tec. He stopped hesitating and fought with himself.

"We will go forward to meet the battle," said Tec. "There are ships in there, fighting something we may never understand or conquer, but we must try hard to remember that all of us feel ultimately alien..."

"Alien!" Jorin was frightened, reminded of his past feeling about himself.

"Shut up, son," said Lorrz.

". . . in the sense that we are all sentient," continued Tec. "So remember this if we have to kill the enemy, because he is one of us."

The ship plunged ahead toward what only it could see.

And out of the darkness came another shape: a monster dragon blocked their way.

"The Roiiss ship," bellowed Uru. "R'ya!"

"You are here," she said in Tec's mind. He opened to let the others share, and Ka asked the question Tec was afraid to ask himself.

"You sense that she is different," said Ka. "Are you afraid?"

Tec did not answer. He punched the controls for ship to ship visiphone. "Please transmit electronically, R'ya."

Her image—purple, vivid, beautiful—filled the viewer. She was R'ya, and yet not R'ya, with a quality of power and splendor in her face and bearing which she had not had before.

"Greetings, Tec," she said grimly. "You have come to witness the death of a galaxy, for Wirzan will succeed in his goal of destruction, as he has before. If you have any power, help us stop him before it is too late."

"Us?" said Uru. "You have allies?"

"Two races in this galaxy are immune to the hyperspace effect and had begun space travel at the time Wirzan took over. They work with us in our ships." She moved aside to reveal silvery animals with blue appendages at the back of her control room, accompanied by others with large bulbous shapes and oddly jointed tentacles.

"I can see Valosians in your ship," R'ya said, "but they are green."

Tec flashed a brief telepathic explanation and asked the question plaguing him. "What do you mean, R'ya—our ships?"

R'ya smiled and vanished, replaced by a view of the outside of the dragon ship, moving in on the *New Ven-*

turer. A balloonlike device emerged from the airlock to clamp down on top of Uru's bubble. Tec saw Uru snake through into R'ya's ship.

The viewer went dark and so did telepathic communication. It was only a few seconds, but it seemed hours to Tec until R'ya's image returned, accompanied by Uru, who suddenly looked grown-up.

"Uru and I are too large for human—as Uru calls them—ships," said R'ya. "We will visit your planets if we conquer Wirzan, but we will probably always be people of the dragon ships, as I and my children have been for centuries."

Tec's gasp of surprise, accompanied by a feeling of loss, brought a squeeze on his arm from Ka's trunk.

"Yes, Tec," said R'ya. "I was pregnant when the humans released me from stasis, but I did not permit the embryos to grow while I was building Valos. Then Wirzan captured me. I suppose he thought he could use me in some way in this galaxy, but I eventually escaped and had six children. Over the years we've built a fleet, but we've never been able to get out of the galaxy, because Wirzan controls the local hyperspace transition. I am afraid you are trapped, Tec, and I'm sorry I've been sending messages."

Uru caressed her folded wings and put the tip of his tongue briefly upon her forehead.

"But I am glad you have brought Uru to me," she said.

"My instruments tell me you have six other ships, R'ya," said Tec. "They seem to be fighting Wirzan beyond that dust area."

"We've been fighting him for many years," said R'ya despondently. "You have only one small ship. How can we ever win?"

"Your ships distracted him enough to permit my control of our computer, so we could enter galactic space here. Now we must try to find a way to stop Wirzan with you," said Tec.

"You try," said R'ya. "I am tired, discouraged. Be in charge, Tec. I feel that your power has grown, but I am afraid that Wirzan's has grown even more. He's learned how to enlarge black holes rapidly by combining and destroying stars, and soon the process of destruction of this galaxy will proceed quickly by itself, and he will go on to the next—to the galaxy I grew up in, where Uru and the humans evolved. We must go far away to some galaxy he will never reach. He is so large now that he needs much energy, but a few local galaxies may suffice and we can carry out our lives elsewhere. I believe it is impossible to destroy him."

"Wirzan must be destroyed," said Tec. "He is not merely killing a few galaxies to provide energy for himself. He is doing the Second Experiment!"

"I don't know what that is," said R'ya.

Tec looked back at Ka and the humans. Lorrz nodded.

"R'ya," said Tec, "Wirzan is killing the universe itself!"

8

Those in Tec's ship, who knew already, watched R'ya realize the horror of it.

"Destroy the universe?" Her scales rippled; her nostrils flared and smoked. "But even he must live in it!"

"There's a twin universe on the other side of hyperspace," said Tec. "The two universes expand and contract alternately. The Roiiss lived in the other universe, living long enough to be exposed to the increasing radiation caused by its contraction. Immortal in an expanding universe, the Roiiss knew they would die when their universe suffered its own death. Then they discovered that energy from the dying universe passed into the twin, causing it to start expanding eventually, producing stars, galaxies, second-generation stars, elements, planets, and life."

"The Roiiss went through hyperspace to the twin?"

"Unfortunately," said Tec, "any direction out of hyperspace leads into one's own universe. The Roiiss went through the fabric of hyperspace in a different way, through black holes. That was the First Experiment."

R'ya shuddered. "I remember our experience, nearly getting sucked in. Then they plan to go through the black hole at this galactic core?"

Tec's analytic centers were clamoring for him to examine the pronoun in R'ya's last sentence, but he was in a hurry. "Wirzan's not going through a black hole until he thinks the other universe is expanded enough for life to exist. Therefore he's starting as many and as big black holes as possible to hasten the death of this universe and the expansion of the next, which he hopes to control completely."

R'ya was silent, and Tec wondered if she understood.

"Black holes," he continued, "are part of the normal development of any universe, ultimately causing its collapse, as matter and energy fall through; but a universe must be allowed to develop in its own time and way. Wirzan must not destroy this expanding universe and the evolving life in it, just to satisfy his megalomaniac thirst for power."

"And the Roiiss?" said R'ya.

"Your—our—people developed sufficient matter control to mutate remarkably, until they could go through a black hole. They put me and your embryo in heavy stasis, heavily shielded, but they wanted to remain conscious and in control during the trip. They paid for that consciousness by becoming so changed and weakened that they could hardly exist in this new universe, especially on planets in the normal protoplasmic way. Remember that they waited millions of years for planets to form . . ."

"Weakened?" asked R'ya. "Tec, please . . ."

"When the last five came to see me on the planet Earth, they blocked my memory and communication centers so that I could not remember or move, even after primitive Earthmen turned off Wirzan's stasis field. The Roiiss, fleeing Wirzan, were so weak that fighting me took their last energies. I've always been sorry they died—strange, rather evil creatures interested only in themselves, but your ancestors and my makers."

"Tec! Listen to me!" R'ya shook her lovely head and rustled her wings. "Follow my ship through this interstellar dust and you'll see that Wirzan is not here alone. He's their robot now. Wirzan works for the Roiiss Elders!"

The small ship followed the dragon ship through the obscuring cloud, emerging in a spattering of stars that moved above the galactic core. Tec had homed in on R'ya's signal almost exactly. The *New Venturer* hung above the spiral-armed, flattened disc of M31.

Ash and Lorrz gasped. Ka trumpeted with fear.

"Is that possible?" asked Jorin, pointing at the viewer.

"It's there," said Tec flatly, trying to conceal his dread from the others. "Therefore it's possible."

It was unlike a black hole resulting from the death of a single star, which may have a disc of light circling its equator as photons are trapped in orbit, slowly spiral in, and are replaced by others drawn from space outside the black hole.

"It's completely black," said Tec, wonderingly, "and enormous."

"As if the entire center of M31 has been punched out from all directions," said Lorrz.

Tec could see Wirzan, now a huge boxlike thing hurling mental and physical energy at the six ships protecting R'ya and her friends. And beneath Wirzan—

"A sleeping dragon," marveled Ka.

"Yes," said R'ya, "very big and very dangerous. Wirzan found the Roiiss and helped them get energy by starting supernovae formation in—the Clouds—I hear the name in your mind, Tec. When I went there in search of Uru, Wirzan persuaded the Elders to put me in stasis. They brought me to this galaxy—alive, because I guess the Elders don't want to kill me yet. But they will when they perform the Second Experiment and leave me behind! No wonder Wirzan decided to take the Roiiss for his masters when he realized they could take him to the next universe!"

The sleeping dragon looked like a monster brooding an obscene egg, thought Tec, for far below was the black hole. Perhaps the dragon was not asleep, but was using all its energy to fight the gravitational pull while gathering some of the energy pouring in from the rest of the galaxy.

"It's a magnificent dragon," said Jorin. "Why does it want to kill everybody?"

"To possess everything," said Tec wearily.

"The universe belongs to all of us," said Lorrz.

"Yes, we must stop them," said R'ya. "I've grown stronger, but I'm afraid even to try to communicate with the Roiiss.

"Someone must," said Jorin.

Tec found he had to resist a temptation to laugh, as humans do under psychological pressure. "Someone must tickle the nose of the dragon—Elders! You are five, not one, but you listen and speak as one. Listen then to me, your robot Tec."

The sleeping dragon stirred only slightly.

"You must listen, Elders. Your new robot Wirzan is using you. He needs a strong master to manipulate into doing what he wants, insuring his survival and supreme power in the next universe, where you will become his slaves . . ."

The telepathic bolt hit Tec harder than he expected, although he'd tried to be ready for it. Pain seared his mind.

"Silence, robot, do not disturb the Roiiss!"

"Your Roiiss, Wirzan?"

"MY Roiiss. I should have killed you long ago, Tec. It was a gross oversight which I will now remedy."

The paralyzing force tore at Tec's brain in spite of all the mental shielding and counterattack he could muster. He saw that no one else on the *New Venturer* was affected.

"Turn your self off, Tec, or I will deactivate you," Wirzan commanded. "I have the strength to do it now, in spite of the battle from R'ya's bastards."

As the paralysis seeped past Tec's defenses, he turned to Jorin and held out his hands in supplication.

"Tec needs help," said Jorin, probing telepathically.

"No, Jorin, don't come inside! Wirzan will find out you are telepathic and turn on you . . ."

"Not on all of us," said Jorin, leaning back against Ka, who was swinging his trunk in an angry rhythm.

Jorin and Ka must have made telepathic contact with every human, because the force of the counterattack almost overwhelmed Tec.

"Get out!" said his friends.

Wirzan withdrew.

"Have we killed him?" asked Jorin eagerly.

"Humans are so primitive," said Ka.

"Wirzan is almost impossible to kill," said Tec. "But there is one creature who might manage." Tec turned his attention to the dragon, who now had one eye open.

"Hear me, Roiiss! I speak to you as life speaks to life."

Tec could feel that his mind was protected by the minds of the humans, Ka, Uru, and R'ya. Fearlessly, he opened his mind so all could sense the telepathic dialogue.

"Are we alive?" asked the dragon sarcastically.

"Not as protoplasmic creatures are, but neither is Wirzan or myself," said Tec. "You Roiiss are alive, because you are intelligent and aware—and you change."

"We do not want to change."

"Ah, is that the problem?"

"Leave us alone, Tec. We want a universe to ourselves. We will destroy the hyperspace boundary and turn both universes into one unchanging, unevolving one."

"That's not possible! Any universe changes—stars evolve, die . . ."

The dragon yawned, shutting its eyes tightly. "Wirzan says he will fix it. The one unchanging universe will be a sea of energy in which we will float forever, never to be disturbed by petty minds like yours."

Tec sent a vivid picture telepathically, past the closed eyelids, directly to the visual centers of the dragon. The picture was a dragon, yawning such a tremendous yawn that it split apart.

The Roiiss opened both eyes.

"Boredom, my Elders. You are bored. You will be bored—forever and ever and ever and ever . . ."

"Stop that!"

"Wirzan has convinced you to want certainty, to want an existence that is easy and completely predictable, because it will be totally under your control." Tec searched for refutation and Margot gave it to him. He resumed, triumphantly, "Simple pleasure and safety are not enough, even for creatures with less complicated minds than yours. There is proof—small, unintelligent animals kept in cages *deliberately* choose difficult but interesting ways of getting food in preference to easy, boring ways."

"We do not care."

Tec paused to think it out. "Do you want a cage of your own making, Roiiss? It will not work. Have you forgotten that to be unchanging is to be dead? Hasn't survival been your goal, through the First and Second Experiments? Don't you still want to live?"

"We will live in our solitary universe."

"No!" Tec had it now. "In organismic growth, in electrical oscillation of living brains—which register electronic patterns even while asleep—the essence of life is constant change."

The dragon was wide awake now, angrily thrashing its tail. "We will control the universe to come. We will continue to be alive, meditating upon the beauty of the cosmos without interference!"

Would they ever understand? "Roiiss," Tec continued fiercely, "you cannot enjoy the luxury of intelligence—or even of being alive—without permitting change in the universe. The very chemistry of life itself—robotic or protoplasmic—is based on continual change, and once you have allowed change anywhere . . ."

"Tec speaks lies!" shouted Wirzan telepathically.

"It's a perfectly obvious fact," said Tec, "but Wirzan did not remind you of it, because he probably hopes you will die peacefully in the peace of the solitary universe, which he will then use for his own purposes, whatever they may be."

"Wirzan," said the dragon, "what do you intend doing with the next universe?"

"Do you want to be a god, Wirzan?" asked Tec.

There was no answer, but the hideous shape that was Wirzan began to grow larger in the viewer as it moved away from the dragon.

"He's going to ram the ship and kill us," said Ka. "I sense the murderous impulse. It's very strong."

"Fight him," said Tec. "All of us must fight him!"

Wirzan's mindshield was up. They could not turn him back.

He hurtled onward like a mindless missile.

9

"Tec!" shouted R'ya. "Get back into hyperspace if you can!"

But this time Wirzan had an unbreakable grip upon the ship's computer. He sped closer, closer, past the ships of R'ya's fleet, tossing them aside like bits of dust. On, on toward the *New Venturer*.

And suddenly, an immense purple claw snaked out as if from nowhere, plucking Wirzan from his chosen path.

"We have not finished our conversation," said the Roiiss.

"Tec is the enemy!" yelled Wirzan. "If you listen to him, you'll have to deal with other intelligences, alien minds that will make you sick."

"That may be true," said the dragon, meditatively. "So many alien minds. Yet you misled us, Wirzan. Tec is right—it is impossible to have both intelligence and an unchanging universe."

"You can have alternating universes completely to yourselves," said Wirzan, "if you cooperate with me."

"How boring," said Tec. "Diversity cures that and incidentally makes ecosystems more stable."

"We do not care," said the dragon.

"You should," said Tec. "You're probably responsible

for the existence of life in this universe, in all its diversity."

"What!"

"It's unlikely that each twin universe, each time, has laws of physics which permit the development of life. Perhaps your entry into the cosmic egg of this universe altered the laws of physics in such a way as to make life possible here. R'ya's survival is proof of the idea that your interference made this universe similar to the old."

"But, Tec," whined the Roiiss, "we do not like the life forms here, and we do not want these creatures to deter us from our private contemplation of the universe."

"You and Wirzan don't realize that diversity is the secret of the universe."

"Secret?" asked the dragon, dangling Wirzan from its claw.

"Each sentient creature sees beauty in a different way. Now, thanks to the R-inclusion that you gave to this universe by way of R'ya, universal telepathy will permit sharing those diverse views . . ."

"Unimportant," sneered Wirzan. "Power is everything, Roiiss."

The claws squeezed a little harder around the robot called Wirzan. "Well, Tec?" said the Roiiss.

"No," said Tec, "power is not everything, although it is needed for the right to create, to affirm oneself. You were once technological geniuses, Roiiss, but you never thought much beyond survival and power. Listen to what I have learned: diversity permits not only sharing of beauty, but it is the way the universe evolves to become aware of itself."

Wirzan's sudden blast of destructive mental power would have killed Tec's mind had it not been protected by so many others.

"Idiot! To tell the Roiiss that!"

"What's the matter, Wirzan?" asked Tec. "Did you

want to BE the entire universe next time?"

The dragon coiled and uncoiled, its huge eyes staring at the creature it held. "Wirzan, you are beginning to annoy us," said the Roiiss.

Wirzan struggled, tentacles writhing. "Kill Tec, you fools!"

"You must die," said the Roiiss.

Tec could not help saying it. "Must he?"

The claws began to squeeze and at that moment Wirzan lashed at the Roiiss with his mind. Even Tec could feel the pain.

The dragon reeled and dropped the robot, which sped past the Roiiss, away from the ships.

"Catch him!" shouted R'ya and Tec.

Wirzan was going too fast. The black hole swallowed him as if he had never been.

The Roiiss seemed to recover first. The dragon preened itself and yawned.

"He was boring," said the Roiiss.

Tec had never been so angry. He pummeled the dragon with a telepathic blast.

"You have grown so stupid, Elders! Do you realize what you have done in letting Wirzan go?"

"Well, you had doubts about killing him, Tec. We suppose you'll say that's our fault, since we programmed you to nurture all life."

"Perhaps Wirzan could have been rehabilitated," said Tec, "but now he has gone through a black hole..."

"Into a cosmic egg," said the Roiiss savagely. "Not even Wirzan can survive that without our help, and even if he did, it will be eons before expansion..."

"Wait," said Tec grimly. "Wirzan guessed the probable truth. There will never be cosmic eggs again. In your First Experiment, you probably changed the structure of hyperspace so that the twin universes alternate differently, starting from less collapsed states. Wirzan may survive until the twin universe is ready for life."

"Indeed?" said the Roiiss. "Then perhaps we were wrong to listen to you. We could have gone with him."

"And controlled him, the way he is now? Never," said Tec.

The dragon snarled, the enormous eyes blazing at the *New Venturer*. "We are angry with you, Tec. You have spoiled everything—you and your stupid diversity."

The pressure mounted in Tec's head as the Roiiss turned their power on him. They had the strength to kill everyone. He did not know what to do so he lashed out intuitively.

"Roiiss! You are not even one creature. You try to use the royal 'we,' but you are five separate individuals trying to avoid the responsibility of affirming your individuality, of developing."

"Developing?" The dragon hissed, its outlines growing indistinct. "What is the use of developing our individual selves? We want to be one creature—and if Wirzan can want to be the entire universe, then so do we!"

"You are five, Roiiss," said Tec relentlessly.

The dragon shivered and shattered, the pieces dissolving into shapeless color.

"Five individuals," said Tec, with pity. "Five pieces of the twin cosmos, five ways of being aware, parts of the whole that someday might—with all the other parts—evolve into a consciousness field. Think of it—sentient universes, grown from the diversity of evolving consciousnesses, each individual contributing something different. Perhaps we've made a real start, now, with the telepathy you made possible, Elders."

The swirling colors wound into five spinning balls, dancing madly above the black hole. Would they enter it?

"Roiiss! You could be so useful, helping smaller creatures through black holes when this universe starts naturally to contract, building the level of consciousness higher in the next universe, sharing the experience of all."

Five dragons coalesced from the spinning balls of color. Five terrified dragons.

"We are afraid, Tec! We are too different now. We cannot find a home; we are so alien. Are you not alien, too, Tec? You are the only one of your kind."

Tec thought about it, sensing that his human friends and Ka, watching him in the control room, were experiencing intense anxiety.

"Yes, I am one of a kind," he said, "while you are five, Roiiss." He smiled with compassion—perhaps, he thought, partly for himself. "I am alien—and alone. Yet so is each sentient creature, and I—like each individual—must discover existence in my own way."

"You have a home with these protoplasmic creatures, if you want it," wailed the Roiiss, "while we have none!"

Suddenly Tec thought he had the answer. "Elders! Perhaps you have changed so much that you are now suited to life in hyperspace, learning to understand that world of the graviton from which normal geometric space-time-energy fields balloon out as universes. If you do, you might be able to create other hyperspaces and new twin universes. You'll have your own homes!"

"And in the meantime?"

"While you're learning about hyperspace?" Tec laughed. "Oh, my Elders, think of the adventure of it! As the R-inclusion is becoming part of the living cells of protoplasmic beings, so you can become living parts of the hyperspace-universe complex . . ."

"Silence!" The five dragons drew closer, disdainfully inspecting Tec's ship like great monsters ready to crush small prey. Tec held his mind quiet, open to whatever the moment would bring. The Roiiss looked back at the black hole, and then majestically swam through space out into the still-living galaxy. Their telepathic words drifted back to Tec.

"An interesting idea, robot Tec. We will think about it." They were nearly out of sight. "And Tec, you had better think about Wirzan. He will be waiting to kill all of us."

"Yes, Elders," said Tec dutifully.

The *New Venturer* came out of hyperspace early to check the navigation. It was alone, for R'ya and Uru had remained for a while in M31, to meet Tec eventually on Roiissa.

"There it is," said Tec. "Home."

The Milky Way galaxy spread across the viewer in a splendor of stars.

Only Ka and Lorrz were with Tec in the control room, since the rest of the humans were preparing to rejoin humanity.

"Roiissa on that rim, Valos across the entire galaxy, and Earth—" Ka paused, his trunk wavering. "Where is Earth?"

"It's a small planet," said Tec, "orbiting an ordinary G-type star—about there." He pointed to a spiral arm and was suddenly homesick for the small beauties common to the eye of a planetbound beholder. The sight of an entire galaxy was too much. He turned back to the ship's controls.

After the *New Venturer* shimmered into and then out of hyperspace once more, they saw a cloud-wreathed planet before them.

"Isn't Earth beautiful!" Ka said.

"A living planet," said Lorrz. "It won't exist forever, so we must enjoy it."

"And protect it while it's there," said Tec, bringing the *New Venturer* slowly through the atmosphere, closer to the continents and seas of Earth.

"Transitory," said Ka mournfully, expressing the sudden, silent grief. "Sometimes I think it's better to be like my ancestors, not intelligent enough to be able to worry."

Lorrz laughed sardonically. "Yes, the future looks so dark that eternity owes us a meaning."

"But the price of awareness is eternal uncertainty!" said Tec, suddenly angry.

Ka swayed from one to the other. "Don't you think there will be futures even if Wirzan fights us from one universe to the next?"

"Even if everything, everybody changes as the universes alternate, until all time ends!" said Lorrz.

Tec watched his two friends as they stared eagerly at the planet that had evolved the life manifested in their cells. But the Roiiss inclusion was there, too—a gift from one universe to another!

Who knows where lines of evolution may lead—or how they may converge?

"Don't worry," said Tec, "there will always be dragons."